Kimberly
and the
Captives

Colonial
Captives
1

Kimberly and the Captives

✗

ANGELA
ELWELL
HUNT

Tyndale House
Publishers, Inc.
WHEATON
ILLINOIS

Library of Congress Cataloging-in-Publication Data

Hunt, Angela Elwell, date–
    Kimberly and the captives / Angela Elwell Hunt.
      p.   cm. — (Colonial captives ; bk. 1)
    Summary: While traveling to America along with a group of kidnapped children in 1627,
fourteen-year-old Kimberly prays for God's intervention when a pirate ship demands
surrender of the children.
    ISBN 0-8423-0328-6 (pbk.)
    [1. Voyages and travels—Fiction.   2. Kidnapping—Fiction.   3. Pirates—Fiction.
4. Christian life—Fiction.]   I. Title.   II. Series: Hunt, Angela Elwell, date–
Colonial captives; bk. 1.
PZ7.H9115Ki   1996
[Fic]—dc20   95-47907

Printed in the United States of America

02   01   00   99   98   97   96
9   8   7   6   5   4   3   2   1

Happy are the poor in spirit,
for theirs is the kingdom of heaven.
Happy are those who mourn,
for they will be comforted.

GLOSSARIES

Parts of a Ship:

aft: behind; toward the stern

bilge: the low point of a ship's hull

bow: the forward part of the ship

bowsprit: a rod extending forward from the bow out over the water

capstan: a spool revolving on a shaft, used to wind the cable that raises and lowers the anchor

companionway: a narrow stairway leading from deck to deck

deck: the floor

fore: ahead; toward the bow

gangplank: a movable bridge for boarding the ship

hold: a cargo area below decks within the ship's hull

mainmast: the largest, center mast on a ship

mizzenmast: the mast nearest the stern

orlop deck: the lowest deck of a ship with four decks

port: the left side of the vessel, as one stands on board ship and faces the bow

starboard: the right side of the vessel, as one stands on board ship and faces the bow

stern: the rear of the ship

yard: a long, slender rod fastened horizontally across the mast to support a sail

yardarm: either half of a yard

Sailors' Terms:

aboard: on board a vessel

ahoy: call to attention

astrolabe: a navigation instrument that measures the altitude of the sun or stars

aweigh: anchors up

ballast: heavy objects used to maintain the ship at the proper draft

bilge rats (slang): boys who work below decks; also called bilge boys

bosun: foreman; officer in charge of the crew

captain: officer who is master or commander of the ship

caravel: Portuguese ship with square sails on her bowsprit and front mast, but lateen (triangular) sails on her other three masts

draft: how far down in the water a ship is

even keel: condition of floating properly upright in water

flotsam: floating wreckage

founder: to take on water to the point of capsizing and sinking; to go nowhere

furl: roll up or take in sails

lateen sail: a triangular sail

make sail: raise sails and set out

reefed sail: a sail partly lowered and secured

rest at anchor: float in position

run before the wind: sail swiftly

sea legs: ability to walk aboard ship, especially in rough seas

swab: to mop the deck

Other Words:

alcove: a recess in the wall of a room

bodice: the upper portion of a woman's dress

breeches (pronounced "britches"): knee-length trousers

cambric: a fine, thin fabric made of linen

camlet: a fabric made of silk and wool

chamber pot: a portable container used as a toilet

chemise: a woman's one-piece undergarment

damask: a silk fabric

indentured servant: one who agrees to be purchased as a servant for an agreed-upon term of years, usually to pay off a debt for sea passage

kirtle: a woman's skirt

knave: a rascal; a false, deceitful person

leggings: a cover for protecting the leg below the knee

magistrate: an officer of the law

phthisis (pronounced "thy-sis"): another name for tuberculosis, a disease that affects the lungs

pray: often used in the seventeenth century to mean "please" or "beg"

privy: a toilet area

save: often used in the seventeenth century to mean "except"

sea biscuit: a large, coarse, hard unleavened bread; also called hardtack

sempstress: a seamstress; dressmaker

soft: often used in the seventeenth century to mean "quiet" or "softly"

swill: garbage and table scraps usually used to feed pigs

vermin: any number of small animals with destructive habits: flies, lice, bedbugs, mice, rats, etc.

victuals (pronounced "vitt-els"): stored provisions or food

"In 1627, 1,500 kidnapped children arrived in Virginia. They came from Europe and some became great successes. A six-year-old, kidnapped by a sailor and sold in America, married his master's daughter, inherited his fortune, and bought the sailor, by then a prisoner."

—*The Encyclopedia of American Facts and Dates*

"I have inquired after the child that was lost, and have spoken with the parents. His name was John Brookes. The last night he was after much trouble and charge freed again, and he relates that there are divers other children in the ship crying, that were enticed away from their parents, that are kept and detained in the ship. The name of the ship is the *Seven Brothers* and as I hear bound for Virginia; and she is now fallen down to Gravesend, and, if a speedy course be not taken to stop her she will be gone. I heard of two other ships in the river that are at the same work, although the parents of the children see their children in the ship, yet without money they will not let them have them. . . . I am confident your mercy to these innocent children will ground a blessing on yourself and your own. Pray let not your great affairs put this good work out of your head to stop the ships and discharge the children."

—From a letter to Sir Anthony Ashley Cooper, April 1668
(from the British Public Records Office)

THE
BEGINNING

Monday, May 3, 1627

1

Kimberly Hollis felt her heart pound when she saw the messenger at her door with a sealed parchment in his hand. "I am looking for Mistress Mary Hollis," the youth said, wiping a layer of dust from his face. "I bring her a letter from a ship at the docks."

"Mama!" Kimberly cried over her shoulder. "A letter!"

Her mother's quick footsteps echoed through the small apartment, and in a moment she stood behind Kimberly. Her delicate face seemed to grow pale as she stared at the parchment in the messenger's hand. "Is the letter from Virginia?" she whispered.

"Aye, ma'am," the young man replied, thrusting the parchment forward. "I've brought it right from the ship's captain."

Mistress Hollis's hand shook as she reached for the letter. "Thank you," she whispered hoarsely. She clutched the paper in her hand and sank onto the bench by the door. "Pay the young man something, Kimberly," she said, her eyes glued to the letter. "Take a shilling from my purse."

An entire shilling! Kimberly didn't argue, but pulled the coin from her mother's purse and placed it in the messenger's grimy hand. With a quick smile and a doff of his cap, he left, and Kimberly shut the door.

"Aren't you going to open the letter, Mama?" Kimberly asked, kneeling on the floor at her mother's feet. "What if 'tis good news?"

"What if 'tis bad?" her mother answered, meeting Kimberly's eyes with her own. "Your father has been gone for so long. . . ."

"Read it," Kimberly urged. As her fingers shook, Mistress Hollis broke the smear of wax that had sealed the letter and unfolded the crinkly parchment. Her voice trembled as she read aloud:

"To my very dear wife Mary:

"Greetings in the name of our Lord. I trust that you and our daughter are well. The days of my service in Virginia have been long and difficult, but, praise God, they are almost at an end.

"'Tis this I propose and hope, dear wife, that you will agree to my plan. I would have you and Kimberly join me as soon as you are able. Sell whatever we have in England, and use the money to purchase passage on a ship to Jamestown in the Virginia colony. By the time you arrive, I will be a free man. And because the colony's charter doth grant fifty acres to a man for each person he brings into the colony, when you and our daughter arrive I shall be granted one hundred acres upon which we can begin our own plantation.

"I have labored long and hard to provide a new life for us, dear wife. I hope this letter finds you well, and I hope that you will soon join me here. My love and prayers are with you both. Do not hesitate to come.

> "Your loving husband,
> "Thomas Hollis"

"He will be a free man," she whispered as she lowered the letter into her lap. "Thank God, Kimberly, your father will be free!"

Kimberly shook her head in confusion. She had been only seven years old when her father left for Virginia, and she could scarcely remember him. For the last seven years she and her mother had lived alone in their tiny two-room apartment in London. It was hard to imagine life with a father, and harder still to imagine life across the sea on a plantation in the wilderness called Virginia.

"Do we have to go?" she asked, her voice a tiny whisper in the quiet of the room. "I'm afraid, Mama. I've heard about the savages and the forest—"

"Your father would not send for us if it were not safe," her mother answered, resting her hand upon Kimberly's golden brown hair. "He left to search for a new life, and selling himself as an indentured servant was the only way he could pay for passage to America. But he's worked seven years and is now free to make his own way in the world. 'Tis a miracle he survived, and 'tis a blessing of God that we will be allowed to join him. Yea, Daughter, we have to go. Your father needs us, and I believe 'tis God's will that we follow him there."

Kimberly paused for a moment, hesitant to say what she was thinking. "I don't know him, Mama," she said, turning her eyes from her mother's happy face. "I don't even remember what he looks like."

"Not remember?" her mother asked, surprised. Then she laughed and patted Kimberly's cheek with her hand. "Of course, darling, you were so young! But you

5

were the joy of your father's life. 'Tis because he wanted something better for you that he chose to go to Virginia at all. London is no place for a man of no money and no position, and it seemed best that we begin life anew in the colony." She leaned back against the wall, and her eyes dreamily gazed far away. "Your father is right handsome, he is. Tall and broad shouldered, with brown hair like yours, and a beard. You always giggled when he kissed you, for the beard tickled your skin. Don't you remember?"

Kimberly shook her head.

"Ah, 'tis no matter. In a few weeks, as soon as we're away from here, you'll see your father again. And then we will be together as a family, and in the New World. One hundred acres! Ah, Thomas, you were right, we would never have had such an opportunity in London! Land is too scarce here, there are too many mouths to feed—"

She sat suddenly upright and pressed her pale hand to her forehead. "So much to be done! We'll have to sell everything as your father suggests, and I'll have to tell Master Walker that I'll be leaving his service. And you'll tell your friends good-bye, for we're off to Virginia."

She stood and moved toward the bedchamber, coughing quietly into her handkerchief. Kimberly sat back on the bench, stung by the news. They were leaving England! For all her fourteen years Kimberly had lived in London; it was the only place she knew. Though she and her mother weren't rich, they were happy and comfortable in the small apartment. But now they would be leaving everything!

A meowing wail at her feet caught her attention, and Kimberly knelt to lift her cat, Gretchen, onto her lap. Kimberly was certain that Gretchen wouldn't be allowed on the ship to Virginia. She'd have to stay behind and catch mice for some other family.

"Lucky you, Gretchen," Kimberly whispered, feel-

6

ing the vibration of the cat's loud purr beneath her hand. "You'll get to catch English mice for the rest of your life."

Gretchen only blinked her green eyes and ducked her head, eager for another caress.

* * *

The sound of her mother's coughing woke Kimberly the next morning. Though it was early May, their small bed-chamber was cold, and Kimberly did not want to leave the cozy warmth of her blanket. But despite the chilliness of the room, her mother had already begun to dress for the day. "Hurry, Kimmie," Mother called as she slipped her kirtle over her chemise. She began to quickly pin the top part of her dress, the bodice, to the long kirtle. "You'll have to dress yourself. I'm off to Master Walker's first thing this morning to tell him that we'll be leaving soon. I want you to come with me, for mayhap you can earn a few pence today running errands for Mistress Walker. We'll need every bit of money we can earn for our trip."

Kimberly sat up in bed and shivered as she blinked the sleep from her eyes. Already things had begun to change! Her mother usually tarried in the morning, tidying the small rooms and arranging her hair in a neat knot at the top of her head. But today her brown hair flew in a thick tumble over her shoulders, and she had barely run a comb through it before she tucked it under her cap. She paused to yank the blanket off Kimberly. "Hurry, girl! The day will not wait for us!"

Kimberly got up from her mattress, knowing better than to grumble. Her mother worked hard all of the time, but now that they had to raise money for a trip to America, she would have to work even harder. Her mother earned enough from her job in Master Walker's pie shop to furnish the small rooms where she and Kimberly lived, but they did not have a lot of extra money for pretty clothes or toys or even firewood. One small log per win-

7

ter day was all they could afford, and Mistress Hollis's cough had begun in the autumn and grown steadily worse over the last few weeks. Kimberly had often thought about writing to her father, but she doubted that he could do anything to help. In seven years not a single shilling had come from Virginia. Kimberly's mother explained that her father could not earn any money as long as he served a master, and so there was none to send. But now that he was free, Kimberly hoped he could begin to earn a living so Mother wouldn't have to work so hard.

Kimberly splashed her face and hands with freezing water from the large washbasin in the room; then she pulled her kirtle and bodice from her trunk. Her outfit was just like her mother's, only smaller. All children wore grown-up looking clothes no matter how young they were, for children often worked in jobs with their parents, just as Kimberly went to work with her mother. Today she hoped to do extra chores to earn money. Perhaps she could deliver Master Walker's pies to the lords and ladies in the large houses in the center of London.

She pinned her kirtle securely, then attached the bottom of her bodice to the kirtle with three pins. After slipping into a clean pair of sleeves, she pinned them into place and then turned and studied her reflection in the still water of the washbasin. She was neat and respectable, if not exactly pretty, and that was all that mattered today.

"Hurry up, Kimberly!" Her mother's voice carried a note of impatience, and Kimberly pulled on her cap and slipped her feet into her heavy wooden-soled shoes. Mother was waiting by the door, a frown on her face, and Kimberly hurried by, determined not to slow her mother down again.

* * *

"Y'are going *where?*" Mistress Walker asked, her eyes wide with surprise. "My heavens, Mary, you can't be thinking to take the child to Virginia. Why, I've heard stories about that place that will curl your hair—"

"My hair's curly enough," Kimberly's mother answered, smiling politely as she pulled an apron about her dainty waist and set to work. "As soon as we've found a ship and raised the money for passage, we'll be on our way, Mistress Walker. I wanted to tell you and the master so you can find another pair of hands to help out here."

Mistress Walker dropped onto a stool as if her legs had given way. "I can't believe it," she said, shaking her head. Her dark blue eyes fastened on Kimberly. "Are you going to let your mother get on a ship and travel across the ocean? She's in no condition to travel. Her cough has done nothing but get worse—"

"I'm fine, Mistress Walker," Kimberly's mother answered, moving to the large wooden table where several bowls of dough waited. Delicious smells from steaming pies were already beginning to rise from the hot ovens. "'Tis just a cough, and summer is on its way. I'll be better in warmer weather, and mayhap the sea air will do me good."

"Mayhap the journey will kill you," Mistress Walker grumbled as she rose to her feet.

But Mary Hollis ignored the older lady's complaining and set to work with energy, stirring flour and milk together. As she worked, she nodded to Kimberly. "The master's still in his room upstairs, dear. Why don't you go up and ask him if there are deliveries to be made?"

Kimberly nodded and scurried up the narrow staircase at the back of the pie shop. At the top of the stairs stood a dark door, and she hesitantly tapped it.

"Who's there?" a hoarse voice called, and Kimberly bent to speak into the keyhole.

"'Tis Kimberly Hollis. My mother bade me ask if there are deliveries to be made this morning—"

The door swung open with a rush, and Kimberly

nearly fell backward as an older man with a heavy belly opened the door and glared down at her. Despite his frown and gruff voice, his eyes twinkled, and she grinned up at him. Master William Walker was all bark and no bite. Though he pretended to be stern and demanding, she knew it was he who left scraps of meat out for the town's stray dogs. And at least once a week he would hand her a nearly empty bucket of milk and gruffly whisper, "Do y'know a cat who likes milk?"

And she would say, "Yea, Gretchen likes milk."

"Well, give it to her then," he'd growl, stamping away. And so she'd take the bucket home, Gretchen would lovingly lick it clean, and the next morning Kimberly would return the freshly scrubbed bucket to the bakery.

Now Master Walker frowned at her from the top of the stairs. "Pies to deliver?" he snapped, taking his pipe from his mouth. "And who's going to deliver 'em?"

"I thought I would, sir," she said, timidly lifting her eyes to meet his. "Since my mother and I will be going to Virginia soon to meet my father, she said we both need to do extra work to earn the money for passage."

A dark cloud passed before the master's eyes; then his face softened, and he stooped down to Kimberly's level. "So you've decided to join your father in America?" he asked, raising a bushy white brow. "Ah, I thought this day might come. Though I'll hate to lose you and your mother, I suppose your place is with your father."

Kimberly swallowed hard and hoped he wouldn't see how afraid she was. She lifted her chin and nodded. "Yea, sir."

"Well, then," he said, scratching his beard. "Lady Burgess did ask for two venison pies, and Lord Norcross has ordered two cherry pies that are ready downstairs. Have the mistress wrap them for you, and you can deliver them if you like. But take care—" he thrust out a stubby finger— "I won't have you hurry and spill them in the streets."

"Nay, sir, I won't," Kimberly said, flashing him a smile. Four pies! Surely she'd be paid well for delivering four pies.

Her heavy shoes clunked loudly on the stairs as she skipped down them, but she could hear Master Walker calling after her, "And mind that you don't stop to talk to any of the street boys! Y'are too pretty for your own good these days, little miss!"

* * *

London was a gray city in those days, especially in spring when the sun often hid behind low-hanging rain clouds. The smoke rising from thousands of fireplaces and cooking hearths hung in a ghostly fog above the sprawling town, and the streets and buildings had grayed to the same pale hue. It was a busy, crowded place, with men and women, horses and carriages, cattle and farmers moving constantly through the streets toward their homes, businesses, or the docks along the river. Kimberly had to be very careful as she carried the four neatly wrapped pies, but by suppertime she had safely delivered all four pies to the kitchen doors of the large and stately homes. By the time she met her mother outside the pie shop, the pocket at her waist jingled with coins she'd received for her good work.

Her mother seemed tired, and fine lines showed around the corners of her eyes as she smiled at Kimberly. "Master Walker gave me an extra shilling for you," she said, proudly displaying the coin in her hand. "You did well today, Daughter."

Kimberly tried not to let her pride show as she fell into step beside her mother. Her feet ached from dodging the crowds of London all day, but her mother had to be even more tired. Working in the pie shop was hot, boring work.

"Are we working again tomorrow?" Kimberly asked.

11

"Nay," her mother said, lifting her eyes to the western horizon. "Tomorrow I will go down to the docks to book passage on a ship bound for Virginia. We'll have to discuss how much it will cost. Then we will have to decide what we should sell and what we should take with us to Virginia."

Kimberly felt a sudden chill. Part of her wanted to be excited about going on such an adventure, but another part of her wanted to stay at home with Gretchen in the tiny apartment on Straight Street. How could she know which part of her was right?

She gathered her courage to ask a question. "Mama?" she asked, shrugging as if her thoughts were not very important. "Do we have to go to Virginia? Now that father is a free man, can't he come back to London?"

Mother shook her head slowly and sighed. "I wish it were that easy, Kimberly. But there are not many jobs here and no way for a man to earn a living. Virginia is the land of opportunity, and your father has given seven years of his life to help us build something better for ourselves. I can't ask him to come back after he's sacrificed so much."

They walked on in silence for a while, then Mistress Hollis slipped her arm around Kimberly's shoulder. "We've been lucky, darling, because Master and Mistress Walker were kind enough to give me employment and pay a decent wage. But they were God's provision for us, and now we must step out in faith. The Scriptures teach that your father is the head of the home, and as he's called us to Virginia, we must obey and follow him."

Kimberly did not answer as they turned into the narrow hallway that would lead them upstairs to their small apartment. *Why would God call us all the way to Virginia,* she wondered, *when he could take care of us just as easily in London?*

* * *

Mother told Kimberly to wait at home while she went to the docks, for the riverfront was no place for a young lady. Kimberly thought privately that it was probably no place for her mother, either, but life had taken a strange twist in the last few days, and nothing was as it ought to be.

When Mistress Hollis arrived home a few hours later, she sank onto the narrow bench by the door and kicked off her shoes. She panted from exertion, and her face was flushed. Kimberly could tell her mother had been coughing, for her breath came in shallow gasps.

But she managed a quick smile for her daughter. "We can take nothing but a small trunk," she said, as if that were the most wonderful news in the world instead of the most upsetting. "No furniture, no pots, no books save the Bible I plan to put in our trunk. I suppose we should wear a sturdy kirtle and bodice, and pack another outfit so we'll have something fresh to wear when we meet your father. I don't suppose there's much use in packing anything else."

"Only one kirtle?" Kimberly asked, her eyes widening in surprise. "And we'll wear the same clothes during the entire sea voyage?"

13

"Apparently everyone does," her mother answered, untying the bonnet strings at her chin. "The passenger trunks are packed far below on the ship, or so the captain told me, so no one can open them until they arrive in Virginia."

"You met the captain? We're actually *sailing*?"

"Yea, on the *Seven Brothers*," Mother answered. "I met with the captain in an office down at the shipyard. The ship leaves in a week, so we'll have to sell everything before we go."

"Everything?" Kimberly looked around at their few possessions. Though their home was small, she had come to love the sturdy kitchen table where they ate and where her mother had taught her to read. At night, by the dim light of a fire in the corner stove, her mother often sat at that table to read the Bible. They owned the teakettle on top of the stove and the ash bucket at the side, as well as a bench, two mugs, and three plates. Beyond, in the bed-chamber, there were two narrow beds of wood and rope, and two thin mattresses of burlap stuffed with straw. Two trunks held all the clothes they possessed. How could these meager possessions be too much to take to Virginia?

"Must we sell even Gretchen?" Kimberly asked, patting her calico cat as she rubbed up against her legs.

"Nay," her mother answered. She smiled. "I thought we'd give her to Master and Mistress Walker. They've need of a good mouser, don't you think? And Master Walker is always needing a cat to rid him of his extra milk."

Kimberly picked up her cat and nodded, then pressed her cheek against Gretchen's soft fur. In seven days, everything would change. Never would she be able to do this again.

* * *

14 The next six days flew by in a rush. Kimberly hardly noticed that the sun had begun to warm London, so busy were they selling everything in the apartment. The man who lived in the small room upstairs bought their table and chair, and the old man who ran the cobbler's shop downstairs bought the bench. Mistress Walker bought Kimberly's trunk and took Gretchen upstairs to live above the pie shop, and the man and woman who planned to move into the Hollis's empty rooms paid an extra shilling for the beds and whatever else might be left behind.

The day before they were to sail, Kimberly picked out her favorite kirtle, a kirtle of bleached linen as crisp and white as an egret's wing, and placed it in the bottom of her mother's trunk. If she would be wearing a dirty kirtle during the weeks of her ocean crossing, she'd want to wear something white and clean when she came off the ship. With the kirtle she placed a clean petticoat and a bodice of blush-color damask with matching sleeves. Pink and white—she hoped she'd make a pretty picture for the father she hadn't seen in seven years.

Her mother thoughtfully considered what outfit she'd put into the trunk, and Kimberly smiled when she realized that her mother loved her father so much that she wanted to look her absolute best for him. Into the trunk she put a clean smock, a French farthingale and petticoat, and a gown of cream-colored camlet lined with white silk. The bodice was embroidered with tiny pink rosebuds, and the sleeves had been slashed so that pink silk was visible through the openings in the full sleeves. Though the dress was several years old, it was her mother's best. And it did not matter how old the dress was, Kimberly realized. Her father had never seen her mother in it.

Mother also placed in the trunk her Bible and the parchment letter they'd received only a few days earlier. A tiny purse containing what was left of their earnings also went inside the trunk. Then Mistress Hollis locked it and put the key on a chain around her neck.

15

She glanced over at Kimberly. "Now I guess we go to bed," she said, her voice a happy hum in the quiet room. "And tomorrow, at first light, we'll carry the trunk down to the shipyards. I'm sorry there's no money to hire a carriage—"

"We'll be all right," Kimberly said, lying down on her thin mattress. It felt strange to sleep without a blanket, but they'd sold their blankets and quilts, too.

She wrapped her arms around herself to keep warm in the chilly room and waited for sleep to claim her.

WEEK
ONE
�֎

Wednesday, May 12

2

Kimberly woke before the sun arose and stirred at the sound of her mother's wheezing cough. The attack was severe, and Kimberly won dered if she should go outside and fetch a bucket of water from the well down the street. Perhaps Mistress Walker was right and Mother shouldn't go on such a long voyage.

But Mother rose from her bed, and her eyes smiled at Kimberly even as she covered her mouth and hurried from the room. After a moment, she returned, her cough-ing under control. "I can't wait until summer," she said, her voice rasping even as she smiled. "The warm sun and sea air will do us both good, don't you think? Now come, Kimberly, dress and eat a bite of breakfast. I've saved us a little of the cold pie Mistress Walker brought us yester-day. I have a feeling we'll need something in our stom-achs to see this day through."

Kimberly gobbled the pie without tasting it, so

preoccupied was she with thoughts of leaving. The little apartment seemed empty without her mother's table and bench, and the night had been far too quiet without Gretchen's steady purring.

When her mother had finished eating, she wiped her mouth with a square of cloth and motioned for Kimberly to do the same. "Well," she said, slapping crumbs from her hands. "I suppose we'd better head out. The new tenants are planning to move their things in today, and we'd best be gone."

Though the heaviness in her chest felt like a huge rock weighing her to the floor so that she could not move, Kimberly nodded. Her mother tied on her cloak and bonnet and moved into the bedchamber. Unwillingly, Kimberly's feet began to follow her there.

Though they could easily lift their small trunk, carrying it down the stairs proved to be more difficult. As they struggled to carry it through the crowded streets of London, Kimberly began to earnestly wish that she had been born rich enough for a horse and carriage. Why was life so unfair? All of the houses to which she had delivered pies earlier in the week had been mansions with several servants scurrying about in the kitchens. Surely the girls who lived inside wore silk dresses, a different one for every day of the week, and traveled with dozens of trunks packed with toys and feathers and fans and hats and slippers and books and pastries! Why were some people born rich and others born with nothing at all?

Her hand began to burn after walking a few blocks, and Kimberly cried out as a blister on her palm burst and the rough leather strap of the trunk rubbed against her torn skin. "What's wrong?" her mother called, setting down her side of the trunk to look at Kimberly's hand. She frowned and shook her head, then showed Kimberly that her own palm was just as raw and torn. "Mayhap we should change sides," she suggested.

"And hurt our opposite hands, too?" Kimberly wailed, blowing on her injured skin.

Mother's eyebrows rose. "Have you a better idea?"

Kimberly frowned, but after a minute she had to agree that she didn't know what else to do. There was always the purse of money in the trunk to hire a carriage, but if Mother had locked it away she must have had a good reason.

"Let's change sides," Kimberly finally agreed, trading places with her mother. Clenching her blistered fist tightly, she lifted the trunk with her good hand and waited for her mother to lead the way.

* * *

Kimberly almost forgot the pain in her hands when they arrived at the docks along the river Thames. Her mother had never allowed her to walk along these docks, and with one glance Kimberly understood why. The place was certainly dangerous, for strange-looking men roamed the boardwalks, and foreign ships from countries that did not follow English law were tied to the docks. Many men called to one another in loud, unfamiliar tongues and made rude whistling noises as Kimberly and her pretty mother passed by. Past the docks the river churned with choppy waves and glinted silver as the sun shone on its waters. But along its banks the river was scummy with greenish brown gunk, waterlogged barrels, bottles, paper, and fabric. Wads of old canvas rotted beneath the shallows, and barnacle-encrusted planks of wood floated aimlessly along the banks and under the docks. The air smelled sour and rancid with the odors of rotting things and low tide.

21

Mistress Hollis walked confidently along the docks, her head high, and paused before a narrow gangplank outside a brightly painted ship at anchor. "Excuse me, sir," she called to a suntanned man who stood nearby on the dock. "Is this the *Seven Brothers?* Captain Blade's ship?"

The man squinted toward Kimberly's mother. "'Tis the *Seven Brothers,* and no doubt," he said, his voice not at all friendly. "Why are you askin'?"

"I've booked passage upon this ship," Mistress Hollis answered, dropping her end of the trunk on the dock. She folded her arms and returned the man's steady gaze. "My name is Mary Hollis, and I paid good money for myself and my daughter to board. Is the ship still sailing today?"

"Aye, we'll be makin' sail in an hour or two," the man said, slowly coiling a rope in his hand. "But I'll tell you this, Mistress Hollis. If I lets you on the ship, I can't be letting you off again until we reach Virginia."

Kimberly's mother blanched. "Why, I've never heard of such a thing."

"Captain's rule," the man answered, still coiling his rope. "If you gets on, you stays on. And your daughter, too. You see, the captain rules the ship on the high sea, not the king nor anybody else. So until ye arrive in Virginia, y'are under the command of Captain Blade, and there's no disputing his word." The whites of his eyes flashed toward Kimberly. "So are ye both agreein' to the captain's rule?"

"I suppose we are," Mistress Hollis answered, picking up her end of the trunk again. "You won't have to worry about us, sir. We've strong stomachs, and we're not cowards. We're not about to change our minds now."

"I didn't think ye would," the sailor answered, moving confidently over the gangplank toward the ship.

As if to challenge their bravery, the narrow gangplank stood before them. It was no wider than Kimberly's shoulders and would be difficult enough to cross when their hands were empty, but now that they were carrying a trunk . . .

As if he guessed their dilemma, the sailor laughed.

"Leave your trunk on the dock," he called, his sharp voice cutting through the whine of the wind.

"Thank you so much," Mistress Hollis answered. She dropped the trunk and held out her blistered hand to Kimberly. "Shall we cross together?"

Kimberly closed her eyes and nodded. This was the first step of a long and difficult journey, but if they could just get aboard, surely everything would be fine. Once Kimberly had a decent bed and a warm blanket, the cold terror in the pit of her stomach would go away.

She grabbed her mother's hand, pasted on a timid smile, and followed her mother out onto the narrow gangplank that reached across the dark and turbulent waters.

* * *

The ship was not as large as Kimberly had imagined it would be, and seamen crowded its decks in preparation for sailing. Kimberly stayed close by her mother as they stepped through the small opening in the ship's rail that led them to the center of the wooden deck. In front of them, a tall, thick wooden mast reached toward the gray sky. Similar masts stood at the rear and the front of the ship, and each mast was crisscrossed with cables and rope and intricately woven riggings that reminded Kimberly of a vast series of spiderwebs. At the front of the ship rose a little wooden room with another deck serving as its roof, and another similar room and deck stood at the rear of the ship.

Was one of those rooms to be theirs? Kimberly held onto her mother's kirtle. She was ready to go wherever her mother led her, but her mother seemed bewildered as well. Mary Hollis stood in the center of the deck, her eyes wide as the men skittered over the rigging like crabs. Finally one of the sailors standing on the highest front deck pointed down and shouted, "Ye two! Get below, will ye? Passengers aren't allowed on the upper deck."

23

"The upper deck," Mistress Hollis whispered, moving in the direction of the man's outstretched finger. "How do we get to the lower?"

As if in answer, a hatch in the floor suddenly flew open before them as a sailor scrambled out. Kimberly could see a series of ladder-like steps leading to a dark place beneath the deck. Her mother turned around and gave Kimberly an uncertain smile as she began to move down the staircase. "'Tis an adventure, isn't it?" she asked brightly, stepping downward as she clung to the wooden railing. "Wait till we tell your father about this."

Kimberly noticed the complete silence around her and looked up. The seamen on the upper deck and even on the riggings had stopped to watch her mother disappear into the opening. *What's wrong?* Kimberly wondered, her heart beginning to pound. *They act as if they've never seen a woman come aboard! But surely there are other families on this voyage!* When her mother's bonnet disappeared, the men resumed their work, and Kimberly turned and followed her mother down the stairs.

Nothing could have prepared her for what she saw when she reached the bottom. The second level of the ship was nothing but an enormous wooden room, with three square windows on each side open to the sea. The tall masts from above cut through the empty space at even intervals, and, farther in the back, another opening yawned in the wooden floor. But it wasn't the size or design of the ship that startled Kimberly and her mother. Crammed into the second deck were more children than Kimberly had ever seen at one time in any place. Boys and girls, large and small, fair and freckled, plump and thin—a roomful of young faces looked to Kimberly and her mother with questions in their eyes.

"What is this?" Kimberly whispered, tugging on her mother's kirtle. "Are these the other passengers?"

"Where are their parents?" her mother asked.

A babble of voices rose suddenly, and the sea of children surged toward them, each one shouting or crying or talking. Kimberly covered her ears and closed her eyes, praying that the moment was a terrible nightmare she could laugh about in the morning. Her mother's voice cut through the din: "One at a time, please! Tell me what's happening here!"

The mob finally quieted, and a tall, thin boy with dark hair and eyes came forward. He wore a tattered, dirty gray shirt that had at one time been white, and torn leggings covered his thin legs below his black breeches. "We've been snatched," he said bluntly, his eyes glued to Mistress Hollis's face. "We're being taken away to Virginia."

"Snatched?" she asked, shaking her head. "From where?"

The tall boy shrugged. "I was living on the streets," he said, as if it were nothing unusual. "I've been an orphan since I was a wee lad, so no one cares. I heard about blokes snatching children off the street, so I followed 'em to see what was up. Next thing I knew, they had me, too, and tossed me with the likes of these brats into this ship."

"You can't think we're all like *him*," a girl said, pressing her way to the front of the crowd. She was short, plump, and pretty, and wore a dress of a silky blue fabric with an abundance of lace at the sleeves and hem. The blonde ringlets of her hair bounced as she pointed a finger at the boy. "He's an orphan and probably deserves this, but what about me? I'm Brooke Burdon. My father's a respected merchant in London."

Mother frowned. "And why are you here?"

"My nanny was out for the day," Brooke whimpered, wiping a tear from her eye. "And the scullery maid left me with a new groomsman. He was supposed to watch over me, and he took me to the park. I saw a strange man

25

give him money, and the next thing I knew, the stranger took my hand and brought me here! He told me my father wanted to show me a ship he was thinking of buying—"

"You didn't scream?" The words slipped out of Kimberly's mouth before she could stop them.

Brooke frowned. "Why should I? I didn't know I was being *kidnapped*, for heaven's sake. Until I found myself down here with this miserable lot."

"This cannot be allowed," Mistress Hollis said, turning to go up the staircase again. "I'll have a talk with the captain myself. He seemed a perfectly reasonable man when I met him—"

A shadow fell across the opening of the staircase, and a dark voice floated down from above. "Mistress Hollis, how nice to see you. I trust you have found our accommodations reasonable?"

"Well, nay, Captain, I haven't," Mother answered, stepping off the stairs. She lifted her face toward the captain and gestured to the children in the room. "You can't take these children away against their will. There's a girl here who says she's been kidnapped, and others whose parents are bound to be looking for them—"

26 "No one is looking for these youngsters," the captain interrupted. Kimberly strained for a look at him, but her mother's bonnet blocked her view of the small opening. "Most of them are riffraff from the streets of London, homeless creatures who would grow up to be pickpockets and petty criminals if they aren't already. We're doing the king a favor by taking them to Virginia."

"But this girl—," Mistress Hollis interrupted.

"The girl is a spoiled brat, and if she doesn't stop her complaining—"

Kimberly glanced at Brooke, who shrank back from the captain's words.

"—I'll throw her overboard as soon as we're at sea.

Now you have made a promise, Mistress Hollis, and now that y'are on my ship I'm afraid I cannot let you off again. Find your place and keep quiet, for y'are under my command, and I'll entertain no argument."

A heavy wooden panel slammed shut over the opening, and Kimberly jumped back, frightened beyond words at the anger in the captain's voice. Her mother's face was pale in the dim light, and after a moment she turned and looked at the group of silent children.

"Well, it seems as though our captain is *not* a reasonable man," she said, pausing to cough softly over her shoulder. Her voice was slightly strangled when she added, "We'll just have to pray that God will have his way with Captain Blade."

Brooke broke out into loud sobs, and several other children began to cry as well. The tall boy glanced at Mistress Hollis in silence, then stepped forward and thrust out his hand. "My name's Thatcher Butler," he said, giving her a shy smile. "I'm pleased y'are going to be with us, ma'am."

Kimberly's mother nodded. A circle of children against one of the walls opened to make room for them to sit down, and Mistress Hollis sank to the floor and allowed her eyes to sweep over the crowded hold. "So many lost souls," she whispered, tears wetting her lashes. "I had no idea there were so many on the streets of London."

27

Kimberly sat next to her mother and nestled into the space between her mother's shoulder and the creaking wooden wall behind them. The journey to America would be nothing like she had expected.

3

The soft whispers of the other children wrapped around Kimberly like water around a rock, and she huddled closer to her mother. Surely this was all a terrible mistake! At any moment the ship's captain would come down the stairs and say this was all a joke and that he didn't truly intend to transport a mob of crying captive children to the Virginia colony. But the minutes passed slowly by, and no one lifted the hatch at the top of the stairs except an occasional curious sailor.

Kimberly felt a shiver dance down her spine. This musty, crowded hold seemed to crawl with children, most of whom wore rags and many of whom were barefoot. Several groups of girls and boys clung to each other as they whispered and cried, and a few lay stretched out upon the floor with their heads in the laps of their friends. Kimberly didn't know how they could be so calm. Just thinking about Virginia made her stomach cramp, and she'd come aboard willingly. If she'd been brought aboard kicking and screaming . . .

"Mama," she whispered, tugging on her mother's sleeve.

"Shh, Kimberly," her mother said, her eyes closed. "I'm trying to think. Leave me alone for a moment."

Kimberly was thinking, too, and her thoughts weren't happy ones. She had never dreamed the ship would be like this—crowded with crying youngsters and reeking with the sour smell of sweat. A boy leaned against the wall near the window, and she felt his eyes on her. When she looked at him, he smiled, and Kimberly stood up and carefully moved toward him over the unsteady floor. Under the curly brown hair framing his forehead, his eyes were friendly.

"Hello," he said, his eyes lighting in interest as she approached. "I hoped you'd come over."

"You did?" Kimberly asked, hugging herself with her arms. She tilted her head and looked at him. "How can you be so calm about this? I'm scared to death, and my mother's very upset—"

"Don't you want to go to America?" the boy asked. "I do. My mother was a servant in a fine house where they constantly talked about the New World. 'Tis a land of riches, they said, and I'm eager to go there."

"You *volunteered* to come aboard this horrid ship?" Kimberly asked, giving him a doubtful look.

"Yea." The boy extended his hand. "My name's Wingate Winslow, and I'm pleased to make your acquaintance."

"Kimberly Hollis," she answered, timidly shaking his hand. "I can't believe your mother would let you come aboard this ship."

"She died last year," Wingate answered, a shadow filling his dark brown eyes. "So, you see, I had to do what I thought was best. When I heard they were filling a ship with youngsters for America, I came down to the docks. The captain took me aboard without asking a single question."

"What about your father?" Kimberly whispered.

Wingate shook his head. "Don't have one. My mother was a lady's maid at Ascot Estate, a fine family's home, and when she died I was left without a place. I lived in Westminster for a time, doing odd bits of work—"

"Who'd you live with?" Kimberly asked.

"No one," Wingate answered, folding his arms. "I lived *on* the streets, not *in* a house. There were lots of us boys living there, and we made a pretty good life for ourselves. The bakery would throw out old bread every week, and there was hot porridge to be had at the church on feast days."

"No wonder America looks good to you," Kimberly said, suddenly feeling very grateful for the tiny rooms she and her mother had shared. They stood for a moment in silence, then Kimberly waved her hand toward the other children in the hold. "Did any of these others live in Westminster with you?"

A grin flashed across Wingate's face. "Yea. Thatcher Butler." He pointed to the tall, striking boy Kimberly had noticed when she first entered the hold. "He was the oldest of us. Told us where to go for food, how to run so the magistrate wouldn't send us to the orphanage, how to pick a pocket. Of course—" Wingate flushed a deep red— "I didn't pick pockets or snip purses. My mother taught me better."

"But Thatcher did," Kimberly said, eyeing the tall boy with suspicion. Not only was she traveling to America on a ship of captives, but some of the captives were thieves!

"Thatcher thought he had to steal to survive," Wingate answered. He pointed to another boy, a thin lad in tattered clothes who lay sleeping on the hard wooden floor. The boy's hand was curled around a battered tin cup. "That's Christian. He's blind and often sang for his supper. People would put copper pennies into his cup, and when he had enough, he'd buy a beef pie for all of us. People love to hear him sing. He has the voice of an angel."

"Really?" Kimberly stared in fascination at the blind boy. "What happened to his parents?"

Wingate shrugged. "Who knows? An old woman called Nettie used to take him in every night, but she stopped coming about a week ago. I'm guessing she died. So Christian didn't argue when the seamen picked him up. I guess they couldn't see in the dark that he was blind." Wingate chuckled softly. "A blind servant! What master will buy him once we reach the colony?"

"Mayhap he can sing there, too," Kimberly offered. "Every person has gifts, Wingate."

"But not every gift is appreciated," the boy answered. He pointed to a red-haired girl who rested her head on the ledge of the open window overlooking the harbor. Kimberly thought the girl looked older than the other children, at least thirteen. Her face had begun to lose its childish roundness, and soon she would be a very pretty young woman. "That's Abigail O'Brien," Wingate said, smiling as he said her name. Kimberly had the feeling that Wingate was particularly fond of Abigail. "She's Irish. She was on her way to work in a sempstress shop, but one of the sailors brought her here. 'Tis said she is very skilled with a needle."

"Didn't she scream?" Kimberly asked. "Where are her parents?"

Wingate shrugged. "Abigail doesn't speak. She couldn't scream, and she can't tell us anything about her parents."

"Can't she write a note?"

"She knows enough to write her name, but I'd wager

32

she never learned anything but sewing," Wingate said. "But I know the captain's thinking he'll sell her for a good price."

"Sell her?" Kimberly asked. A warning bell rang in her mind. "Y'are not slaves, that you should be sold—"

Wingate gave Kimberly the kind of smile an older person gives to someone who's less experienced in the ways of the world. "Where have you been, girl?" he asked, his voice mildly mocking. "Have you not heard of the indenture? We're all to be sold into indentured service. We'll work for our masters until we're twenty-one; then we'll be free to farm our own land and make our own way in America."

"Of course I've heard of indentured service," Kimberly said, blushing. She thought of her own father, the stranger she was on her way to meet. He had worked as a servant for seven long years, but he was an adult when he made his decision to sell himself into service.

"Surely you don't want to do this," she whispered, placing her hand on Wingate's arm. "If none of you has a choice, this is all terribly wrong."

"In truth, I'm not complaining," Wingate said, shrugging. "Life in a home with a master couldn't be harder than life on the streets of London without a roof over my head. And look 'round here." He pointed to a young boy and girl who leaned against the wall. The girl's strawberry blonde head was nestled against the boy's shoulder, and he rested with his head on hers. "Those two are Denni and Daryl Fortier. They're French, and they don't speak much English. Captain Blade found them in a slave market in Italy. Some pirates had pulled them from the waters as a French ship went down, and their parents of certain are dead. Isn't it better that they serve for only a short time rather than be sold as slaves in a foreign land?"

Kimberly couldn't answer. She stared, openmouthed,

33

at the two cute children, so helpless and innocent looking. Pirates! A sinking ship! What stories they had to tell!

Wingate nudged her arm and nodded toward a dark-haired boy who sat at a window across from the silent Abigail. The boy's eyes were serious and focused as he stared across the water, and Kimberly thought she saw his lips moving as though he chanted a silent song.

"That's Ethan Reis," Wingate said, lowering his voice. "He's a Jew. I don't know where the captain picked him up."

"What's a Jew?" Kimberly asked, whispering.

"Someone different," Wingate answered. "They're strange people. I've heard that the Jews killed Christ."

Kimberly paused. Her mother had often read stories about Jesus from the Bible, and it seemed to her that the *Romans* had ordered Jesus' crucifixion. But Wingate seemed to regard Ethan with suspicion, and the other children had left a noticeable space around him.

The sound of heavy footsteps on the staircase interrupted her thoughts, and a tall, balding man with a sunburned face came lumbering into the hold. He wore a bandanna tied around his neck and a gold ring in his ear, and his dark eyes flashed around the room and came to rest upon Kimberly's mother. "Excuse me, ma'am," he said, his voice gravelly in the stillness of the hold. "But the captain says we'll be raising the sails in an hour or two. So if you'd do us the favor of keeping the brats quiet until we're at sea, we'll have dinner soon after we're underway."

"Keep them quiet?" Mistress Hollis said, her eyes widening in surprise. "And how am I to keep them quiet, sir, when y'are taking them from their homes and loved ones?"

The sailor grinned without answering, then climbed the stairs again. After a moment, a heavy trapdoor fell over the opening, blocking the stream of sunlight from the upper deck.

"That was Squeege," Wingate said matter-of-factly. "The captain's bosun. 'Tis his job, I think, to keep us out of trouble."

"How long have you been aboard the ship?" Kimberly asked.

"Two days," Wingate answered. "The captain's done a good job of filling the hold in that time. You and your mother, of course, were the last ones brought aboard. We were all glad to see your mother—" his eyes softened as he turned to look at Mistress Hollis—"since many of us have never had one."

Wingate's words rang in Kimberly's ears. Never had a mother! Why, her mother had always been at her side! They worked together, ate together, studied the Bible together, and slept in the same room. Kimberly's mother had taught her how to read and bake, how to hem a kirtle and pin a bodice, how to kindle and bank a fire so that it would burn throughout a freezing winter night. If these children did not have mothers, how had they learned to do anything?

She felt a tiny tremor of jealousy. No matter how badly these other children wanted mothers, they couldn't have hers. It was bad enough that she had to give her father to America; she didn't intend to give her mother to a shipload of poor captive children.

But just then a little girl not more than five years old began to whimper in her sleep, and Kimberly's mother crawled forward on her hands and knees and drew the crying child into her lap. "Soft now, be quiet," Mistress Hollis murmured, running her fingers through the child's tangled curls. "Y'are all right. Y'are safe. God will not forsake us."

Kimberly realized that, like it or not, she would be sharing her mother with an entire shipload of captives.

* * *

Kimberly sat silently and chewed on her thumbnail. It was a nervous habit she'd developed during the winter, when her mother ran a fever and began to cough. Since her mother's cough had not disappeared, Kimberly's bad habit hadn't either. As she fidgeted and chewed, Kimberly tried to think. She did not want to go to America on a ship crowded with orphan children, nor did she want to share her mother. She wasn't even sure she wanted to rejoin her father. Why couldn't they stay in England and keep working for Master Walker at the pie shop? At the thought of the pie shop, Kimberly's stomach rumbled and cramped in hunger, and she realized that there was no kitchen in the hold. How were they going to eat?

She gathered her courage and stood up to look for a kitchen but nearly lost her balance as the ship rolled gently beneath her feet. She'd have to get used to walking on a moving ship, unless God's mercy provided a way out. Suddenly hope gleamed like a lantern in the darkness.

Surely there was some way to get off this ship before it left the docks! They wouldn't have to go anywhere if the authorities knew about the captain's kidnapped cargo. If only she could get word to someone in a position of power . . .

She hurried back to the place where Wingate sat on the floor. "Can you swim?" she whispered, looking toward the open window as she dropped to her knees beside him. "If you were to jump out and land in the water, could you swim long enough for me to call to someone on the docks who could pluck you out of the water?"

"Heavens, nay," Wingate said, shuddering. "I've never had my entire body in water, and I never want to."

"Welladay, if you are not brave enough," Kimberly taunted.

"It has nothing to do with being brave," Wingate said, wagging his finger at her like an old woman. "It has to do with being *wise*. We don't know *what's* in those waters."

Kimberly sighed and looked around the hold for someone strong and daring enough to try the escape she had in mind. Finally her eyes came to rest on Thatcher Butler. Ignoring Wingate, she stood up and walked to the small alcove at the rear of the chamber where Thatcher sat. He had been talking to several other boys, but the group fell silent when she approached.

"Can you swim?" Kimberly blurted out, forgetting all the other things she wanted to explain.

"Maybe I can," he answered, giving her a mysterious half smile. "Why do you want to know?"

"I was thinking," she said, glancing around to make sure her mother wasn't listening, "if someone jumped out of the window and called for help, we could tell the authorities that Captain Blade is taking kidnapped children to America. And then people would stop him, and we could get off this ship."

"I'm not interested," Thatcher said, looking away. He began to talk again to his circle of friends, and Kimberly stamped her foot in frustration.

"Not interested?" she said, raising her voice. "Not interested or not brave? One would think that you'd be a leader here, being that y'are older and bigger than most of the others."

His dark eyes met Kimberly's. "Who says I'm not a leader?" he said, his words clipped. "Maybe I am. And maybe most of the older ones here don't mind going to America. Life on the streets is the same, whether in London or in Virginia."

Pretty Brooke Burdon had come over to listen, and she began to wail in earnest at Thatcher's words. "I don't live on the streets," she cried, her face brightening to a cherry red color. "I live in a perfectly respectable house on Eton Court, and my father would be furious to know what's happening to me—"

"Then why hasn't he come to look for you?"

37

Thatcher interrupted. "Why hasn't he sent the police around? Why did your nanny's friend get rid of you in the first place? 'Tis because y'are a brat, Brooke Burdon, and I wish they'd never brought you aboard this ship. Y'are always whining and complaining and bragging about the fine things you have. Well, most of us don't care about any of those things. You wouldn't last a day livin' on the streets, and I've spent seven years there without a word of complaining!"

Brooke whimpered under Thatcher's angry words, and Kimberly almost felt sorry for the girl. Brooke's chin quivered as real tears wet her lashes, and Kimberly realized that Thatcher had spoken the truth. But he had been harsh, and he had no right to be mean to Brooke just because he didn't like her.

"Are you going to swim for the dock or shall I?" Kimberly asked, tossing the challenge over her shoulder as she walked toward the window. Someone caught her kirtle and tugged at it, and Kimberly looked down to see Abigail's wide green eyes. The pretty mute girl shook her head and pointed to the waters below.

Kimberly stepped to the edge of the window and looked down. The deep, dark water seemed much farther away than she had thought possible. And though the docks were crowded, no sailors or passersby moved about where the *Seven Brothers* was berthed. If she jumped overboard, she'd have to swim quite a distance before she'd even be near a passerby, then she'd have to stay afloat, scream, and wave her hands to get someone's attention.

Could she do it? Like Wingate, she had never been swimming in her entire life. She'd never even had a bath. Water was for splashing on the face and hands, and occasionally for wiping dirty arms and legs with a pat of soap. To be covered it in entirely, like a fish—that was beyond imagining.

She shuddered and moved away from the window.

She couldn't do it. Her mother would faint if she did. Besides, *she* wasn't kidnapped. She'd have to convince Thatcher to jump, but she knew he'd have to be well rewarded before he'd consider it. And she'd have to hurry. Soon the captain would make sail, and then there would be nothing they could do.

She walked to the corner where Brooke sat blubbering. Instinctively, she put her arm around the sobbing girl. Brooke lifted her tear-streaked face in surprise.

"I know how sad y'are feeling," Kimberly said in a calm, quiet voice. "I'm sad, too. I don't want to go to America. And I have a plan to stop the ship, but first I have to know something. I think you can help me."

"How can I help?" Brooke asked, hiccuping through her sobs.

Kimberly gave her a tight smile. "If someone were to swim to shore and reach your father, would he be willing to fetch the magistrates down here in time to stop Captain Blade? If we could reach your father, he could save every child aboard this ship. He could find homes for them and see that they had decent clothes—"

Brooke's eyes widened in horror. "My father? Oh, my goodness—well, he'd—," she stammered. "I mean, he'd take me off the ship, if someone could find him in time, but I don't think he'd want to stop Captain Blade. What would he do with all these children? 'Twould cost so much to feed them all, and where would we bed them down for the night? 'Twould be asking a lot of my father."

Kimberly fell silent, understanding more than Brooke had intended. "Your father wouldn't even come to save you, would he?" she asked gently.

"Yea, he would," Brooke said, her chin quivering again. "But he's out of the country. He travels a lot for business, and he's always away. I don't know where to find him, and we couldn't reach him in time. 'Tis not that he wouldn't save me if he could, but I haven't seen him in over a year, and I don't know how to reach him—"

"I understand," Kimberly answered. She gave the girl's shoulder an affectionate squeeze. Even though she had lived in a big house with servants, Brooke was just like all the others in this ship. She had no mother or father, either. Her parents had left her behind like a pretty china doll and wouldn't even miss her until they came home and discovered her empty place inside their fancy house.

"I'll pray for you, Brooke," Kimberly said, moving toward her own mother.

Sudden rumbling sounds thundered overhead. "Weigh anchor!" a strong voice called, and footsteps pounded on the deck above as sailors hastened to obey the captain's orders. A wide, round pole at the back of the children's chamber creaked and began to turn, and Kimberly realized that it was part of the capstan, the stout timber around which the anchor cable was wrapped.

Sounds of creaking cables and flapping canvas drifted down from above. Ropes flew through the air outside the windows, and the London docks began to slowly slip away. Seamen on both sides of the boat called out numbers as they measured the channel so the ship could safely move through deep waters, and from within the belly of the ship many captive children began to cry in fear.

Several of the younger ones ran to Kimberly's mother and clung to her. Kimberly fought her own rising fear and painted on a confident smile as if she sailed across the great ocean every day. She left her mother with the little ones and took a seat next to Wingate, who silently watched the world he had known slide by outside the windows.

"Thus it begins," he said simply, and Kimberly gave him a curious look.

"What begins?" she asked.

"Our adventure," he answered.

4

London disappeared from sight as the captives' ship moved down the Thames toward Gravesend and the North Sea. Kimberly turned from the window as the trapdoor leading to the upper deck lifted, and a strong stream of sunlight flooded the area around the staircase. Squeege descended, a vague smile upon his face, and again he walked toward Kimberly's mother. "After you, ma'am," he said, sweeping his cap from his head as he stood before her.

"And where are we going?" Mistress Hollis asked, shaking the little ones in her lap so they'd wake.

"Dinner, ma'am. Paying passengers first, so the captain says."

Mistress Hollis gave the sailor a confused look. "And where do we eat?"

The seaman pointed toward the yawning hole in the rear of the hold. "The aft companionway will take ye to the next deck. The bilge rats should have our victuals ready by now."

The other children stood from their places in expectation, yet every one of them waited respectfully as Kimberly's mother led the way to the companionway. She peered down into the dark hole, then turned and stepped gingerly onto the stairs.

"Careful now, ma'am," Squeege cautioned. "We wouldn't want you to slip and hurt yourself."

"I can assure you," Mistress Hollis replied firmly, "that I am not about to be hurt."

Kimberly watched proudly as her mother disappeared into the lower hold. She didn't seem at all afraid of whatever might happen, and Kimberly decided that whenever she felt afraid, she'd just imitate her fearless mother. Holding her head high, she walked confidently forward and followed her mother down the staircase into the dark lower hold.

* * *

The *Seven Brothers* was a ship of four levels: the upper decks, where the sailors lived and worked; the passenger deck, where the children were quartered; the cargo deck, where meals were served and cargo was stored; and the orlop deck, the lowest, darkest, nastiest deck of the ship. Wingate explained the ship's layout and construction to Kimberly as they stood in line for their dinner, and he shuddered when he pointed to the square planking that covered the hole leading to the lowest deck. "There's rocks and heavy sand down there for ballast to keep the ship upright in the water," he said. "But you don't want to go down there. Ever. There's rats and roaches enough where we are, but vermin positively rule the place down there. And when it rains, all the dirt and filth from the other decks gets washed down to the orlop deck. Even lifting the trapdoor yonder will release a stench strong enough to sicken everyone in this room."

"I believe you," Kimberly said, crinkling her nose.

The deck where they were standing smelled far worse than the deck above. It wasn't hard to imagine the lowest deck as a terrible, foul place.

Kimberly was surprised to discover how meals were served aboard ship. Huge, dark barrels lined the walls of the windowless deck below the children's hold. In the center of this third deck stood a pile of sand, and in the sand gleamed the embers of a slow-burning log. A black iron pot was suspended above the flames, warming some food inside. Three pale boys, not more than twelve years old, cooked and served the meal. A single lantern swung from a rusty nail in the wooden ceiling, and in the dim light the three boys looked as sickly as ghosts. "Are they captured children like you?" Kimberly whispered to Wingate as they neared the boys.

"Nay," Wingate answered, frowning. "The sailors call them bilge rats. They've chosen a life at sea, I suppose, and stay down here in the third hold. 'Tis their job to cook and clean and do everything the captain tells 'em to do. I think they want to be sailors when they grow up."

"*If* they grow up," Kimberly whispered, noticing again how unhealthy and thin the boys were.

As the passengers and crew of the ship filed past a small table, one of the boys handed each diner a plate and a mug of water drawn from a barrel. When she received her plate, Kimberly took a quick breath of utter astonishment. Upon the tin circle in her hand lay a mounded glob of flour, a small slab of beef jerky, and a spoonful of some dark, warm runny substance that had begun to seep into the floury biscuit.

43

"Is this what we eat all the time?" she whispered to Wingate as they moved to find an empty place to sit.

"Heavens, nay, this is the good stuff," Wingate answered, stuffing a bit of the dry biscuit into his mouth. He paused to swallow the thick lump. "I heard Squeege say that we get hot meals only three times a week, and I'd wager this is a celebration because we're properly under-way. Most days we'll get bread and water, if we're lucky. And the meat won't last long, if it lasts at all. There's no way to preserve it for our entire voyage."

Kimberly felt her heart sink. She missed Mistress Walker's beef pies and cherry pastries more than she could say.

She sat on the floor next to her mother and lifted the beef jerky to her mouth. It was salty and tough, but it was food, and she knew she shouldn't complain about it. Still, she missed the little table in their apartment, the warmth of their stove, and Gretchen's contented purring. Their little home now seemed like a mansion, and Kimberly closed her eyes to pretend that she was sitting on the bench in her own house, eating a slightly stale pie from Mistress Walker's ovens.

* * *

Brooke Burdon closed her eyes and pushed the plate away when the serving boy offered it to her. "Ugh! I can't eat that!" she said, screwing her face up into the worst expression she could produce. "'Tis terrible! I can't eat a biscuit without honey, and I want chicken, not whatever that is. My nanny says I have a tender stomach, and I'm not to crowd it with rough foods like this."

"If y'are not going to eat, Brooke Burdon, move away so that others can." Thatcher's voice cut through the gloom of the hold, and even Brooke was startled by his statement.

"I can't eat it," she said, her eyes welling up with tears. Why couldn't anyone see how miserable she was? "I'll get a stomachache, and then I won't be able to sleep. And then I'll have ulcers or something, and there's no doctor here to take care of me—"

Several boys laughed, but Thatcher crossed his arms and glared at Brooke. "I pity you," he said, scowling at

44

her. "Now stand aside so those of us who appreciate food can fill our stomachs."

Brooke stepped out of the line and waved her hands helplessly. "But what am I to eat? I've got to have *something.*"

Thatcher took the plate offered him and moved away without glancing back at her. "Give the captain your order," he called over his shoulder. "Tell him you want lamb and kidney pie. Strawberries and cream for dessert. And milk for your lily-white complexion."

Brooke gave the back of his head her most furious look. She knew he was making fun of her, but she didn't know why. Why couldn't the captain give her a decent meal? Surely somebody had fruit and soft bread aboard the ship! The captain surely didn't eat this terrible food.

And then she saw him. Captain Blade himself came down the stairs and stood in the back of the line. The other seamen jostled each other, each taking the same food from those ghastly looking serving boys, and then the captain reached the serving table. . . .

Brooke caught her breath, unable to believe what her eyes were seeing. *The captain ate the same food as everyone else!*

Maybe Thatcher was right and there was nothing else. She had to eat this or nothing.

She'd choose nothing. She raised her chin, about to climb the staircase, but then her stomach tightened, and she knew she'd be starving by morning. She'd get sick if she didn't eat something. And even though the slop those boys were serving was likely to turn her stomach, dry bread was better than nothing.

Still holding her head high, she went through the line again and accepted her plate without comment. Sitting alone on the floor, she nibbled at the disgusting biscuit, tasted the slab of salty beef, and sipped at the stale, warm water. This wasn't anything like the food she

45

had at home, but it would have to do until she was res-
cued or the captain returned her to London. Aboard this
ship she was like a silk dress among burlap rags, like a
diamond in a coal mine. She didn't belong on a ship destined for America, and she was determined not to stay.

* * *

After dinner, the passengers and crew climbed back to
their respective places. Kimberly sat against the wall next
to her mother and leaned her head against the sturdy
planking of the ship. The sounds of the seamen overhead
gradually stilled, and she imagined them lying down upon
the deck to sleep, wrapped in pieces of canvas or an extra
sail.

The reddish pink glow of sunset shimmered on the
waters outside as the sun slipped slowly into the horizon
ahead of them. Her eyelids grew heavy with the gentle
rhythm of the ship. How many nights would she pass like
this before her journey would come to an end? Wingate
had told her the voyage might take anywhere from six to
twelve weeks, depending upon the winds and weather. No
matter how long it took, Kimberly had the feeling that
she would leave the ship far older than when she had
entered it. She already felt like she had aged a year in just
a day.

Mistress Hollis coughed softly, and Kimberly urged
her mother to lie down. After a moment of resistance, she
did, and immediately several of the younger children
came to pillow their heads in the soft folds of her kirtle.
The soft, regular breathing of children slowly filled the
cabin, and Kimberly watched the sea and sky and thought
about what she had left behind and what lay ahead.

A sag-bellied rat skittered across the floor in search
of food. Kimberly was tempted to throw her shoe at it,
but paused, afraid she'd hit one of the sleeping children
by mistake. After a moment, the rat stopped, sniffed the

air, and disappeared into a hole in the floor. Kimberly sighed in relief and leaned back against the wall. Only the creaks and groans of ancient timbers and cables disturbed the stillness, and Kimberly imagined that she and God were the only two souls awake on the ship. It was easy to imagine that the people aboard the *Seven Brothers* were the only people alive in the entire world, so isolated did she feel out on the black water.

5

Kimberly! Wake! Y'are having a nightmare."
Her mother's hand shook her shoulder; her
eyes were clouded with worry. Kimberly
blinked as a rush of relief swept over her. She
was safely on the ship beside her mother. Thin streams of
early morning light came through the windows, and she
could hear the reassuring flap of the canvas sails overhead.

But still she shivered. "What a dream," she whispered, reaching out for the reassuring touch of her
mother's arm. "We all had to walk the plank. And I could
see Virginia, and 'twas burning, with Indians hiding in the
bushes and buildings—"

"Soft, Daughter, you'll frighten everyone," her
mother said, but a smile lay behind her eyes. She ran her
fingers over Kimberly's tousled hair. "'Tis morning. Why
don't you see if there's someplace where we can clean up a
bit?"

Kimberly nodded and rose to obey. But after one

quick walk around the crowded hold, she knew it was silly to think that Captain Blade's ship might have something so necessary as a washbasin.

"I'm sorry, Mama," she said, kneeling to sit in front of her mother. "There's nothing to wash in."

"I had dared to hope," her mother answered, offering her a smile. She held out her arms, and Kimberly nestled close to her. "But we can endure anything for just a few weeks. This will all be over soon, and then we'll be with your father."

Kimberly closed her eyes as the dark fears of her nightmare pressed down upon her again. She couldn't shake the feeling that this trip was a mistake, that they shouldn't have come. But how could she make her mother understand?

"Mama," she said, slowly opening her eyes, "maybe we should pray and ask God to make the captain turn the ship around. You said yourself that 'twas wrong for the captain to take these children to America. After my nightmare, I'm beginning to think 'tis wrong for us to go, too. What will we do when we get there? We have no place to live, nowhere to go—"

Her mother's eyes blazed with inner fire. "Kimberly Hollis," she said in the tone of voice she always used when Kimberly said something she shouldn't have. "Can you be losing your courage at this late hour? Your father sent for us, and we're his family, so we're going to join him. And God has provided for us thus far, so I'm certain we're in his will. And though I don't know why the Almighty has chosen to put us here with all these children, still, 'tisn't my place to question whether or not I might do some good. We're here according to God's will."

Kimberly knew there was no point in arguing. No matter how real and terrible her dream had seemed, her mother wouldn't understand. Though she hadn't seen him in seven years, Kimberly's mother was in love with her husband, and she would be willing to travel to America on a whale's back if she had to.

Mistress Hollis paused to cough into a handkerchief. When the spell of coughing had passed, Kimberly noticed that her mother seemed very pale and tired.

"Mama, you should rest," she said, pulling away. "I'll try to keep the other children quiet so you can sleep."

"I'm all right," her mother whispered, lying back upon the floor. She rested her head on her thin arm, for she had no pillow. "If the little ones are lonely, tell them to come to me. I think I can still remember how to tell a story or two."

Kimberly nodded and moved away.

* * *

England itself disappeared from sight as the captives' ship moved through the English Channel and finally into the great western ocean that lay between England and America. Kimberly's stomach knotted as all signs of land faded from view. The wind-whipped waters of the ocean rose up and snarled at her when she walked by the open window, and the faces of the children around her tightened into grim, serious expressions as they realized they were held afloat only by a fragile boat of timber and nails.

51

Kimberly tried not to think of stories she had heard in the pie shop. This was an age of exploration upon the seas, and the men and women of London loved to gossip about daring sea captains and brave explorers. Some customers had talked about great sea battles between the English and Spanish. Ships could be sunk by a single well-aimed cannonball from a Spanish ship, the customers had assured Mistress Walker. Others spoke of disease that stalked those who traveled the oceans, killing women and children by the dozens before the ships arrived in their ports of destination. Other people talked of ghost ships that appeared in the mist and vanished in the light of the morning sun. If you see a ghost ship, you are doomed to sink in the deep, or so the stories said. Other visitors had spoken of sea monsters—giant whales and squids and creatures of the deep that could wrap their tentacles around a ship and pull it to the bottom of the ocean before the passengers knew what had grabbed them.

Kimberly used to delight in such tales. Her skin would prickle into gooseflesh, and the hair on the back of her neck would lift in tingles of anticipation. But now the words of those stories came back to haunt her, and she wished she had never listened. As her eyes roved across the gray green ocean, she wondered what a whale really looked like. Could one actually swallow a ship whole? And if it could, could she remain alive inside long enough to be spit up onto dry land like Jonah in the Bible story?

As her mother slept, Kimberly moved to the corner where Wingate sat with his head resting on his knees. He must have been napping, for when she sat down he widened his eyes and jerked his head as if she'd startled him.

"I didn't mean to wake you," she said, tucking her kirtle around her legs as she pulled her knees up. "You can sleep if you want to. I told my mother to rest—she doesn't look so good today."

52   "Could be seasickness," Wingate said. His voice was husky. "Or sometimes people nap just because there's nothing else to do. Sleep makes the time pass more quickly."

"Will we get breakfast?" Kimberly asked, looking toward the dark door that led to the lower deck.

Wingate laughed. "Nay. We get one meal a day, usually at midday or later, depending on the weather. If a storm blows in and the captain's busy on deck, we'll be lucky to eat at all. 'Tis just as well. Anything a body eats in a rough storm soon becomes an offering to the sea."

Kimberly crinkled her nose at the thought of losing her dinner. The hold smelled bad enough when the children were healthy; how could they bear it if everyone became sick?

"I have been praying that God will turn the ship around," she abruptly told Wingate. "My mother doesn't agree because she wants to join my father in Virginia. But she's not well, Wingate, and I think she needs to go back to England. We had an apartment there, and she had a job, and we had friends. Things would be so much better if we just went home—"

"Who are you thinking of when you say that?" Wingate asked, interrupting her and lifting one eyebrow like an old man. "Are you thinking only of yourself?"

Kimberly threw her head back, surprised and hurt by his rebuke. "I'm thinking of you, too! Surely you don't *want* to be sold into indentured service! And Brooke didn't want to be kidnapped, and I don't want to face savage Indians—"

"But your mother wants to see your father, and the captain wants to make his money, and I want to be off the streets of London," he said. His voice gentled. "Think, Kimberly, about those of us who weren't as fortunate as you. Virginia couldn't be as bad as London for folks like me and Thatcher and Christian. We had no homes at all, nor clothes in the freezing winter, nor food unless we begged it. Disease roamed the streets, and 'tis likely we'd soon be dead from the pox or some other illness if we stayed in England. London is no place to be alone. We faced dangers and evils you can't begin to imagine." He looked at his dirty hands, and his eyes deepened with some secret sorrow. "I speak truly, Kimberly Hollis. London is no place for children. At least in Virginia we can have masters, jobs, and hope for a future."

"But I had something in London!" Kimberly wailed, unwilling to think about what Wingate had said. "I had a cat, a lovely calico called Gretchen. And though we sold everything so we'd have a bit of money on the trip, if the ship turned around we could go back and use the money to set up our house again! And Brooke could go home if she wanted, and then you and the captain and whoever wants to could leave for Virginia. But 'tis wrong for the captain to take people who don't—"

"Ye had money?" Thatcher's voice suddenly boomed from a crowded corner, and Kimberly felt her stomach tighten. At that moment Thatcher had the shifty-eyed, hard look of a thief. She did not doubt that he'd been a pickpocket, and probably a very good one.

"We did," she answered, giving him a quick glance. "A wee bit. But 'tis all locked tight in our trunk."

"Your trunk?" The slight suggestion of a smile showed at the corner of Thatcher's mouth. "And where do you suppose that trunk is?"

"Why, 'tis—" Kimberly paused. She and her mother had come aboard the ship and left the trunk on the dock, hoping one of the sailors would bring it aboard. Surely someone did! But where did he put it? It wasn't on this deck, nor had she seen it on the lower deck, where the food supplies were stored. Unless the captain had kept it on the upper deck or slipped it below while she and her mother slept.

54

"That trunk's been emptied of its goods and tossed into the sea by now," Thatcher said, leaning back upon an elbow. His dark eyes raked her face as she sputtered helplessly. "I know sailors. You and your mother came aboard, and 'tis likely the seamen on the docks took your trunk."

"Nay! 'Twas brought aboard, I'm sure," Kimberly said, feeling her face grow hot. "It had to be brought aboard. It had everything we own in it—our money, our clothes, Mama's Bible—"

"It never left the docks," Thatcher answered confidently, looking up at the ceiling. "I saw it with my own eyes. 'Twas sitting on the decks when we cast off our anchor. You can't expect things to be done for you, miss. You should have known that."

Kimberly covered her face with her hands. What was she going to tell her mother?

6

Envy twisted in Brooke's heart as she watched Wingate pat Kimberly's shoulder in pity. Why didn't anyone feel sorry for *her*? Kimberly and her mother had *chosen* to come on this wretched ship, but *she* had been kidnapped! And the other children—street rats, really—thought that America was going to bring them all the riches and food and nice clothes they'd never had in England. Well, Brooke Burdon could tell them a thing or two about nice things! Her house had been one of the finest in Eton Court, and she had trunks and wardrobes filled with silk dresses and petticoats and hats and ribbons and stockings. And as for food—well, her father employed three cooks, each one determined to outdo the other two. At her house she had enjoyed breakfast, dinner, supper, and teatime, with lots of snacks in between. Sweets, treats—whatever she wanted, whenever she wanted it. And now it wasn't fair that she was on this stinking ship! And it *especially* wasn't fair that this new girl should receive pity and make friends when she, Brooke, was far prettier and more lady-like.

Brooke lifted her chin and smoothed her hair, looking around for someone who might be her friend. Ethan, the Jewish boy, sat by the window as always, his eyes fixed on the water as if his mind were a thousand miles away. She didn't want anything to do with *him*, for she'd always heard that Jewish people were different, though she didn't exactly know how. Thatcher sat alone in a corner, his dark eyes calculating some mischief, and the sight of him gave Brooke the creeps. Denni and Daryl were cute and charming, but they didn't understand much English, so they wouldn't be able to comprehend all that Brooke wanted to tell them. Christian sat alone in the center of the room, Brooke's favorite spot, but he was blind so he wouldn't be able to appreciate how pretty Brooke was. Abigail and Wingate were firmly affixed to Kimberly's side, and a host of other children were too young for Brooke to bother with. Who would be her friend and listen to her tale of woe?

Finally she made her choice and walked over to the center spot where Christian sat. Almost playfully she tapped the rim of his tin cup with her fingernail. "If we were back in London, I could fill this cup with gold shillings," she said, looking carefully at the boy for the first time. It was a pity he was blind, for he had nice blond hair and delicate features that reminded her of a dressmaker's china doll. His pale green eyes stared past her at nothing.

"What good would gold shillings do me?" he asked, lifting one shoulder in a shrug. "Someone else would only take them out and replace them with copper pennies."

"Ah, but gold can do a lot of good," Brooke said, sinking to the floor next to him. "My papa used it to buy a big house. And we have lots of servants to take care of us when Mama and Papa are away. There are three cooks in my house, and my nanny, and the butler, and the groom for the horses, and the stable boy—"

"I know you," Christian answered, a shy smile lighting his face. "You are Brooke."

"You've heard of me?" she asked, her heart lifting.

"I've heard you," he answered, pressing his lips together as if he tried to keep from laughing. "You've done nothing but complain ever since you were brought aboard the ship."

Brooke clenched her fist in anger. How dare he say that about her? "And why shouldn't I complain? I was taken from my house—"

Christian held up a hand. "I've heard the story," he said quietly. "And I know that your heart is broken because your mama and papa don't even know y'are gone. How long has it been, Miss Brooke, since you've talked to them?"

"They were home at Christmas," she began. "You know, my papa travels a lot—"

"I said since you've *talked* to them," Christian interrupted, his voice heavy with pity. "Don't you ever talk to your parents?"

Brooke caught her breath in surprise. How could this boy know anything about her? But it was as if he'd opened a window of her heart and looked inside. His pale, sightless eyes seemed to understand why she cried so often, why she threw temper tantrums to annoy her nanny and frustrate the maids. She only did it so her parents would come rushing home from their travels and take care of her. What she wouldn't give to talk to her parents now!

But she couldn't let the others know what her home was really like. They thought she was rich and powerful and loved. She couldn't let them know she was as scared and helpless as a tiny baby.

59

"You don't know anything," she said, turning up her nose at Christian. She stood and flounced her kirtle in his face before she realized he couldn't even see her; then she stomped toward the window. Imagine a poor beggar boy feeling sorry for her! If she were at home and Christian were begging in front of her house, she'd tell the cook to call him in, let him smell the savory pies for dinner, and then cast him out without even a scrap! Or maybe she'd bake him a pie filled with hay from the horses' troughs—

"Why did Christian make you angry?" A new voice interrupted Brooke's thoughts, and she looked down to see Ethan Reis looking up at her. He had dark, curly hair and wide brown eyes and would have been cute, she thought, if he had been a regular person.

"None of your business," she snapped, folding her arms across her chest. "How could a beggar boy make me angry? I'm angry at the captain, and at Miss High and Mighty over there with her mama."

Ethan's eyes flew to the corner where Kimberly and her mother rested, then he looked back at Brooke. "The Scriptures say there is a time for anger and a time to mourn. I think this is a time for thinking."

Brooke snorted. "I'm tired of thinking. What is there to think about on this ship?"

Ethan's mouth twitched in a half smile. "God. My parents told me that we ought to often think about the Master of the universe."

Brooke stamped her foot. "God isn't going to help us. Do you think God was around when I was kidnapped? He wasn't. And he's not going to hear your prayers, either. I heard Kimberly tell her mother that we should pray for the captain to turn the ship around—"

"He could do it," Ethan said, nodding as he looked out the window. "God can do anything. Nothing is impossible for him."

Brooke stared at the boy in astonishment. "You

60

really believe God would turn this ship around?" she said, raising her voice. Several of the other children turned from their conversations to stare at her. She felt their burning eyes and laughed. "Well, let me tell you something! God won't convince the captain to turn this ship, but I will!"

She turned to face the crowd of children. "I'll show you all," she said, lifting her chin. "You wouldn't help me get off the ship in London, and I'll not help you once we get back to England. I'll tell my papa about all of you, and you'll be thrown into the poor people's prison. They lock beggars up, you know, especially if they steal things!"

She ended her speech glaring at Thatcher; then she turned on her heel and ran to a quiet corner to think. What would it take for the captain to return to London? An emergency, perhaps, or a storm. Or if he thought he was losing his mind—

She grinned. What had her nanny always said? "Brooke Burdon, y'are going to be the death of me yet! Y'are driving me out of my mind!"

Brooke smoothed her curls and smothered a smile. She knew just how to get the captain to turn the ship back to England.

61

* * *

Kimberly wiped her mother's hot forehead with a corner of her kirtle. Her mother had slept all morning, restless and weak, and awoke only to cough in deep, rumbling breaths. Worry burdened Kimberly like a heavy cloak upon her shoulders. How could she help without medicine or a doctor? And how could she find the courage to tell her mother that they would have no money, no clothes, and not even the family Bible when they landed in America? All they owned now were the clothes they wore, and after many weeks at sea, those clothes were sure to be soiled and worthless.

Kimberly felt her chin begin to quiver as she sponged her mother's sweaty forehead. Would she and her mother be beggars when the ship finally reached land? Would they be thrown into the prison for people who couldn't pay their debts? Even if Brooke did manage to convince the captain to return the ship to England, Kimberly had no money for a doctor to help her mother and no money to rent a place where they could live.

Kimberly's thoughts were interrupted when a shadow fell across her face. Startled, she looked up. Thatcher stood in front of her, a scrap of cloth in his hand. "'Tis part of my old blanket," he said, thrusting the cloth toward Kimberly. "Give it to your mother for a pillow. 'Tis not right that she should have to lay her head on the hard floor."

Kimberly accepted it, surprised, and did not comment as she rolled it into a small round ball and placed it under her mother's head. Thatcher knelt down at her side, and Mistress Hollis's eyes fluttered open for a moment at the touch of the soft fabric upon her fevered cheek. "Nice," she whispered, smiling her thanks. "I'm just so tired. . . ."

62 Her eyes closed again, and Thatcher moved away, leaving Kimberly alone to wonder what sort of boy he really was. He seemed so tough, so reckless and confident. Yet there was a soft side to his nature, or he wouldn't have given up the only scrap of blanket on the ship.

* * *

The stomping of heavy boots above told the children it was dinnertime, and after the seamen had crossed through their chamber and descended into the lower hold, the youngsters followed, hungry for anything the bilge boys might serve. There was no hot gruel today, only a hard, floury "sea biscuit" and a wooden cup filled with stale-smelling water. Kimberly accepted both without comment, grateful for anything to put into her rumbling stomach. The sails above made soft, snapping sounds in the breeze as the sailors and children filled their bellies. Then a crash and a high-pitched whine broke through the stillness.

"I won't eat it! I won't eat such swill! 'Tis garbage!"

Brooke Burdon stood in the food line with her hands upon her hips. Her tin plate lay on the floor at her feet; her wooden cup rolled lazily across the floor in the slow rhythm of the rocking ship.

Kimberly caught her breath. What was Brooke up to now?

A crowd of seamen parted, and the children gasped when Captain Blade stepped forward. His tanned face was flushed with anger, and his dark eyes snapped as he stared at Brooke. "You will eat whatever you are given," he said, his lips curling into an angry smile. "I want you nice and plump when we reach Virginia, so I can command a good price for you."

"I won't eat anything," Brooke said, folding her arms as she thrust her lower lip forward in a pout. "You can just take me back to England. You don't want a starving girl aboard your ship, do you?"

The captain lifted a bushy brow and for a moment Kimberly thought he would laugh. "You are young and foolish," he said, gesturing to Squeege. "I've sailed upon ships where men nearly died because there was nothing to eat, missy. You should be thankful that we have food at all. Y'are going to eat the bread you were given."

"I won't."

Squeege came out from behind Captain Blade and stomped toward Brooke. "Seein' as though the captain has put me in charge of the lot of ye children," he said, his eyes roving over the crowd, "I'll let you handle this amongst yourselves." He pointed to Thatcher, and then to Wingate. "Ye two fellows will hold our fine lady's arms.

63

And you—" Kimberly grimaced when his finger pointed at her—"you will hold our lady's nose until she opens her mouth for air. We'll make her eat."

Kimberly stood up slowly, unhappy about participating in Brooke's forced feeding. Thatcher and Wingate came forward as if they'd been waiting for a chance to teach the whining Brooke a lesson. Firmly they wrenched Brooke's arms from her hips and held them tight.

"I won't eat this horrid stuff," Brooke screamed at Squeege. Her pretty blue eyes flew toward the captain's. "If you have a pastry or something, mayhap I could eat that."

The captain shook his head. "No pastries," he said, almost smiling. "You will eat the biscuit you threw on the floor." He turned his head and looked at Kimberly. "Pick it up, will you, miss?"

Kimberly knelt on the damp, dirty floor and fumbled for the plate and biscuit Brooke had thrown in her fit of temper. The biscuit was smudged with dirt, so Kimberly wiped it as best she could on her kirtle and held it out toward Brooke.

"Uh-uh," Brooke said, pressing her lips firmly together. Her ringleted curls bounced as she shook her head.

64

"Her nose," Squeege commanded, pointing.

Kimberly felt the eyes of all hundred captives upon her as she extended her hand, and Brooke's eyes crossed as she watched Kimberly's fingers descend. Once Kimberly had firmly squeezed Brooke's nose, the younger girl's eyes closed and she stubbornly puffed out her cheeks.

"One," someone began to count.

"Two," the chant continued.

"Three." Brooke didn't budge.

"Four." Squeege scratched his beard.

"Five." Brooke's face began to redden.

"Six." Thatcher leaned forward with a taunting grin.

"Seven." Kimberly's eyes met Wingate's, and she knew he was wondering how long Brooke would keep them waiting.

"Eight." Kimberly closed her fingers around the stale biscuit. What was she supposed to do, stuff it in Brooke's mouth? She'd have to give the girl time to breathe.

"Nine." Brooke's eyes flew open.

"Ten." Brooke opened her mouth in a gasp, and Kimberly waited until she knew Brooke had taken a breath, then she pressed the edge of the biscuit into Brooke's open mouth. Brooke's eyes met Kimberly's, and Kimberly could see that Brooke had given up. She'd eat, but she wasn't about to go down without one last protest.

Brooke took a big bite, then spat it at Squeege's feet. "Why, you—," he began, but then she leaned forward and took another bite from the biscuit in Kimberly's hand. When he saw that she had surrendered, Squeege halted.

Captain Blade gave the children a victorious smile. "See that ye all eat and are thankful for the food set before ye," the captain told them in conclusion. He climbed the stairs, and the seamen followed, and gradually the children returned their plates to the bilge boys and followed the men up the stairs.

Kimberly lingered in the lower hold for a few minutes to watch Brooke. The younger girl was frowning as she ate, but she was eating, so perhaps she'd be quiet for the rest of the journey and let them rest.

"I'm glad you decided to eat, Brooke," Kimberly called as she moved toward the stairs. "I didn't want to force you."

"I have to eat," Brooke said, wiping crumbs from her mouth on her sleeve. "I learned that yesterday. But I thought maybe I could convince the captain 'twould be better for him to turn the ship around than continue with me on his nerves. He won today, but I'm going to beat him yet. This ship is going back to England, and I'm going home."

Kimberly almost said, "I want to go home, too," but her mother wanted to go to America, and so did many of the others. She couldn't decide whether to wish Brooke well or tell her to accept the fact that they would probably never see England again.

Friday, May 14

7

After a long, tiring night on the hard, wooden floors, Kimberly sat up and hugged her knees. Daylight had begun to stream through the open windows where Ethan Reis knelt in his usual position. Kimberly wondered if he had even slept at all. The boy looked like a statue, for his eyes studied the distant watery horizon as if he could read a world of meaning there.

Kimberly tiptoed past her mother and the sleeping children and joined Ethan at the window. The fresh sea air cleared her brain of the cobwebs of sleep, and she took a deep breath before turning to study Ethan. She knew so little about Jewish people—would he think her stupid for asking questions?

"Good morrow," she said, giving him a polite smile.

Ethan nodded and smiled shyly. His curly brown hair was damp with humidity, and she had the feeling his soft, watchful eyes missed nothing.

"I heard that you are a Jew," she said, feeling awkward and foolish. "And I wanted to know some things and hoped to ask you before the others awoke. But you'll probably think I'm foolish for asking."

"*Lo ha-baishan lomed,*" Ethan answered, nodding.

Kimberly made a face. "What?"

Ethan smiled broadly. "'Tis a Hebrew proverb. 'The shy person does not learn.' If you want to know something, you must find the courage to ask."

"I see." She leaned her elbows on the wide wooden sill of the window and looked out over the water. "How did you come to be on this ship, Ethan? There aren't many Jews in England."

Ethan shook his head. "I have asked the Master of the universe the same question," he said, his voice soft. "I was with my family on a ship sailing from Spain, but I was separated from my parents and sister in a crowd at the London docks. After many hours, a man offered to take me to my parents, and I gave him my hand." Ethan's eyes grew sad as he stared out across the sea. "Instead of taking me to my father, the man sold me to Captain Blade. And now my parents look for me somewhere across these waters."

68   His voice faded away, and Kimberly felt her heart twist in pity. "Is that what you do when you sit here at the window?" she asked gently. "You think of them?"

"I pray for them," he said, "and I wish I had learned the *kaddish.*"

"The kaddish?"

"A mourner's prayer," Ethan answered. "A Jew is supposed to recite the kaddish every day for eleven months after the death of one of his parents. The prayer is supposed to help us." He shook his head. "I don't know why."

Kimberly fell silent. She knew nothing about Jewish people, so she certainly couldn't help Ethan with his kaddish, but maybe there was something else she could do. "When Mama and I pray," she said, turning her head to look closely at him, "we ask God to comfort those who have broken hearts. Isn't that what the kaddish does?"

Ethan nodded.

"Well, I'll pray with you," Kimberly said, rising to her knees. "Every morning, if you want me to. Mama says God answers prayers, so I know he'll comfort your parents. Maybe he'll even make a way for you to find them again."

Ethan nodded soberly. *"Baruch Dayan emet,"* he said, and when he saw Kimberly's puzzled face, he interpreted: "'Blessed is the Judge of Truth.' 'Tis another way to say that the Master of the universe knows what he's doing."

"Yea, I suppose he does," Kimberly whispered. But did he? Why had God put her on this ship? As she began to pray in her own words for Ethan and his heartbroken parents, she realized that she still had a lot to learn about trusting God, the Master of the universe.

* * *

Mistress Hollis was awake and sitting up when Kimberly went back to their corner of the hold. Her mother's face was drawn and tired, but she put out her hand and patted Kimberly's cheek affectionately. "How did you sleep, dear?" she asked, her voice a thin whisper in the noisy chamber. "I saw you talking to Ethan. He seems like a nice boy."

"He lost his parents at a port," Kimberly said, snuggling close to her mother's side. "A stranger offered to help Ethan find them but sold him to Captain Blade instead."

Mistress Hollis shook her head. "I wonder what has hardened our captain's heart in this way. We will have to pray for him, Kimberly. I hope God will change his heart before we reach Virginia."

69

At the mention of Virginia, Kimberly's empty stomach knotted. More than ever she didn't want to go to Virginia. Brooke wanted to go home; Ethan longed to return to England to search for his parents; and her mother needed a doctor. Since they were only three days out of England, why couldn't the captain turn the ship around? Kimberly didn't think any of the children could change his mind, but mayhap he would listen to her mother. After all, weren't she and her mother paying passengers?

Kimberly took a deep breath to say what she'd been thinking. "Mama, I think we should go back to England," she said, turning to look directly at her mother. "Most of these children shouldn't be on this ship, and we'd all be better off in a civilized place, not in the wilderness. And you need a doctor, Mama—"

"We have no money for a doctor, dear."

Kimberly felt as though the floor had suddenly dropped out from beneath her. "You know?" she asked, her voice a narrow squeak. "About the trunk?"

"I know it wasn't put on the ship," her mother answered. "I realized it not long after we came aboard. But a captain who wasn't about to allow us out of this chamber of certain wasn't going to let me go ashore to fetch a trunk. And his seamen were busy with their work—" She broke off in a fit of coughing.

"But our money!" Kimberly whispered, bending close. "We have nothing without that trunk!"

"We have your father to take care of us," her mother answered when she had recaptured her breath. "He will provide for us in Virginia. And what your father can't provide, God can."

"But you need a doctor, Mama!"

A smile flickered across her mother's tired face. "I needed a doctor months ago, Kimberly, and Mistress Walker sent one to see me. I know what this sickness is—

70

'tis phthisis. There is no hope for me no matter where I go." Her voice gentled. "'Tis one reason I knew 'twas right to join your father. I can go to heaven in peace knowing you are with him."

Go to heaven? Merciful skies above, was her mother *dying?*

"Mama, you are not that sick," Kimberly said, forcing a smile. "You have bad days and good days, and as soon as we get you off this ship you'll be better."

Mother shook her head. "Nay, Kimberly, do not fool yourself. The physician in London was honest with me, and I must be honest with you. And I would not have you be distressed, for I am taking you to your father."

Kimberly turned her back on her mother, unable to believe what she had just heard. Her mother was dying, and she had known it for months! They weren't making this trip to America so the family could be together, but so her mother could die in peace!

"You'd leave me?" Kimberly whispered, not turning around. "Just like that, you'd leave me?"

She felt her mother's frail hand on her arm. "I'd never leave you, Kimberly, had I the choice. But the Scriptures tell us there is a time to be born, and a time to die. I'm prepared to meet God." Her voice took on a wistful note. "I miss my Bible, but the Word of God is hidden in my heart. You will miss me, Kimmie, but you will never be alone. You must trust that God has brought us to this place in his timing and for his reasons."

Deep, strong emotions clotted in Kimberly's throat, and she couldn't answer.

"God is calling us to America in faith, and we have taken the first step," her mother went on. "We cannot turn back. We should not even look back, Kimberly, or we can never be happy in the future. Promise me that you won't talk again about returning to England. For better

71

or worse, we're bound for Virginia, and our lives are in God's hands."

Kimberly closed her eyes in an effort to hold back the tears. She had just heard the most chilling, horrifying news of her life, and yet her mother talked as calmly as if they were discussing what sort of dress Kimberly should have from the sempstress's shop.

"Promise me?" her mother asked again.

"I promise," Kimberly croaked, unwillingly. Then she turned and threw herself into her mother's out-stretched arms and let the tears flow. Tomorrow she'd be strong if she had to be, but though she was fourteen years old and nearly grown, she suddenly realized how much she needed her mother.

* * *

Kimberly helped her mother down the stairs for dinner, and after a meal of biscuits and dried beef (which even Brooke ate without complaint), Mistress Hollis looked stronger. When they had all returned to the upper hold, she leaned against the center mast and gathered the younger children around her to tell them tales of Virginia. She had read books, she told them, tales written by the fearless and famous explorer John Smith. He wrote that Virginia was a land of Indians and wilderness, fascinating animals, and fertile fields. Tobacco had long been the richest crop, but planters were discovering other uses for plants that grew wild in the forests.

"For years there were no women in Virginia," Mistress Hollis said, smiling at the girls around her, "but about seven years ago the great London Company began to bring young ladies to Virginia to marry the planters there. Now there are many plantations with masters and their ladies, with many servants to take care of the crops. Each of you, no doubt, will work on such a plantation or in a grand house, and when you are twenty-one, you will be free to marry and work your own land."

"Is there really so much land?" Thatcher asked from the back of the room. "If people keep coming, how can we know there will be land remaining for us when we're twenty-one?"

"America is a vast and unexplored place," Mistress Hollis explained. "And though Englishmen have been pushing their way into the wilderness, they have not yet crossed the lot of it. There is plenty of land for all, and you should not worry that you will not have your chance to work it."

"When I am twenty-one," Wingate said, resting his head upon his knees, "I will marry a pretty woman and have a fine house."

Mistress Hollis smiled. "You are wise to wait until your term of indenture is done before marrying. Serve your master well, for if you do not he might add additional days or weeks to your time of service. But when you have served your term, you will be entitled to a new suit of clothes and a cow. The laws of Virginia also state that you will be given fifty acres of land for each individual you bring over from England."

"So you will own one hundred acres?" Brooke spoke up, the light of respect glowing in her eyes as she looked at Mistress Hollis. "Is that a lot? Is your husband rich?"

Kimberly's mother blushed. "Nay, we're not rich, except in the fact that God has given us a treasure of life and happiness. But my husband is waiting to take care of us, for he has served seven years to make his life in Virginia. And you, my young friends, can make good lives there, too."

"I don't understand why anyone would want to leave England," Brooke said. "London is a beautiful city. England is a powerful country. Why would anyone want to live in the wilderness with a lot of savages?"

"There are many reasons men and women leave our England," Mistress Hollis answered. Her eyes took on a faraway look as she spoke. "In the beginning, some men were driven by the desire to spread the gospel of Jesus Christ. Others wanted to find the riches of gold that Spain had discovered in the New World. Everyone wanted to explore the seas and discover a new sailing route to China. But as time passed and the Jamestown colony was established, people began to realize that England is a crowded place. Your family might be wealthy, Brooke, but most families are not. There are too many people and too few jobs. Disease often sweeps through the city, and too many children have no place to live. The colonies in the New World might solve many of England's problems."

"By giving us a place to live?" Wingate asked. "And jobs?"

Mistress Hollis nodded. "The tobacco planters desperately need men to work the fields. And as tobacco is transported back to England, English workers manufacture goods that the colonists in Virginia need. Our navy has grown strong as we navigate the great western ocean. And you should not fear the savages, for relations with the Indians have improved. They have taught our people many things."

She stopped to cough, and the children waited respectfully until she had caught her breath. "I won't lie to you," she said, her voice much weaker when she spoke again. "Virginia can be a very dangerous place. Five years ago my husband was living in Jamestown when the fierce chief Opechancanough tried to kill every Englishman in Virginia. The chief nearly succeeded, but the people at Jamestown were warned about the attack by an Indian boy not much older than many of you." Her eyes passed over the group and lighted for an instant on Thatcher's face. "No matter how young you are, you can make a difference. It may well be that God has a wonderful purpose in sending you to Virginia. No matter how great the injustice that has been done to you, I pray you will forgive and seek God's help and strength. He will lead you from this time forth."

From where she sat, Kimberly prayed that her mother was right.

* * *

Brooke wrapped a curl around her finger as she listened halfheartedly to what Kimberly's mother was saying. The woman was trying her best to make them feel better about being stolen away, but Brooke didn't want to hear such talk. Mistress Hollis's words droned on in the distance as Brooke concentrated on the next phase of her plan. Her hunger strike hadn't worked. Not only had the captain forced her to eat, but Brooke had been so hungry that she realized she'd never be able to starve herself. Even though Squeege and the captain had won the first battle, they were a long way from winning the war. She had to hurry and think of something. With every day that passed, they slipped farther and farther away from England.

Brooke reviewed the little she knew about ships. Seamen steered by a compass, she guessed, and they probably had maps. Where would they keep them? She scratched her head, trying to remember what she'd seen of the upper deck when she was brought aboard. She hadn't been paying much attention as the man helped her across the gangplank and lured her down into the hold, but she remembered a lot of rigging, ropes, and two small rooms, one at each end of the ship. Surely one of those rooms held the captain's things. Wouldn't a captain always want to know where he was going?

She smiled and pillowed her head on her knees. · From the sounds that came down from above, she knew

75

the sailors were busiest in the mornings and in the early evenings, just before sunset. She'd wait until the hottest part of the afternoon, when sailors and children alike were drowsy in the heat of the day; then she'd sneak up that staircase and take the captain's maps and anything else she could discover. He wouldn't be able to find America when she had finished, and he'd have to turn back for England. He wouldn't have a choice.

Brooke was so proud of her plan that she actually flashed a smile toward Kimberly Hollis.

* * *

Mistress Hollis lay down for a nap, and many of the smaller children lay down near her, their hands reaching out to touch her kirtle, as if they wanted to reassure themselves that a mother was close by. Kimberly sat in one of the corners of the hold, talking in a quiet voice to Wingate and Ethan, and Christian sang quietly in another corner to Abigail and Thatcher. Denni and Daryl, the twins, lay sleeping with their arms tossed around each other, and small groups of other children lay clustered over the floor.

Brooke tiptoed to the stairs that led to the upper deck. Silently she climbed, taking care that her slippers made no noise on the wood. Suddenly she felt a hand close around her ankle.

She looked down. Thatcher stood below her, his dark eyes bright with mischief. "What are you doing?"

"'Tis none of your concern," she answered, angrily shaking her foot to free herself.

"Y'are going to get into trouble, aren't you?" Thatcher asked, an eager smile upon his face. "Do you need help?"

Brooke paused. "And why would you be wanting to help me?"

The older boy shrugged and gripped the staircase

railing. "I'm bored. And y'are not as clever as you think y'are, Brooke Burdon. You could use my help."

"Why should I trust you?" she hissed.

Thatcher put his finger across his lips and jerked his head back over his shoulder. "Soft, or you'll be alarming the others."

"Why should I trust you?" she asked again, her voice low. "Y'are the one who held my arms and forced me to eat the swill they call food."

"Who else are you going to trust?" Thatcher answered, and Brooke realized he had a point. Besides, he was strong, and the door above her was heavy.

"All right," she said, looking up. She continued climbing until she reached the hatch; then Thatcher came up behind her. His strong hands caught the door and lifted it. Brooke held her breath, afraid he'd send it crashing to the floor of the deck. But Thatcher held the door halfway open, just enough for her to slip through.

"Good," she whispered, peering out of the opening. She looked left and then right. Several seamen lounged on the deck, their backs propped against piles of rope or barrels, but most had their eyes closed for an afternoon nap. The others watched the sea or the sails, probably dreaming of where they'd been or where they'd like to be. No one saw her. Carefully, moving with the silent steps she'd learned in years of playing tricks on her nannies, Brooke crawled out of the opening and skittered, crablike, toward the small room she guessed to be the captain's cabin.

The wooden door was ajar, and she slipped into the chamber without a sound. The room was tinier than she'd imagined, with only a bed, table, and bench as furnishings. But on the table stood a solid-looking compass in a wooden case, and under the compass rested several sheets of parchment. Maps.

Brooke could hear her heart pounding in her ears as

she stood over the table. An open window brought in the breeze, and without thinking she picked up the compass and dropped it out of sight through the window. A small, faint splash reached her ears and she realized that others might have heard it, too. She scooped up the parchments in her arms and, sheerly from spite, took a moment to crumple them up in her hands before throwing the wadded parchments out the window.

She hung her head out for a moment and watched the breeze catch the paper balls. They wafted slowly downward, dancing on the wind past the sides of the ship, and finally landed upon the surface of the gentle ocean. They bounced once, twice, thrice, before the waters claimed them, and Brooke paused a moment to let the sun shine upon her face. The sun felt wonderful upon her skin, so *warm*—

A rough hand closed around the back of her neck, and Brooke let out a frightened squeak as someone pulled her back inside. "Cursed be the day I paid ten pence for you!" a rough voice roared. Suddenly the captain's dark face was inches from Brooke's, and his eyes were red-hot with anger.

"Ten pence?" she managed to say, determined that he shouldn't see how frightened she was. "Is that *all?*"

"I'd pay ten shillings to be rid of you," the captain snarled, pushing her toward the doorway. Squeege stood outside, and his thick arms caught Brooke just before she would have hit the floor. "Can't we throw her overboard?" the captain asked, looking out the window for his lost compass and maps. "No one would care. The others would be glad to be rid of her, and I'd of certain sleep better at night."

"You can't do that, Captain," Squeege answered, glaring at Brooke. "She's a pretty lass, and anybody who doesn't know her will pay a good price once we reach

Virginia. And there's a certain man waiting for his money. . . . "

"I know, I know," the captain said, sighing as he turned back to look at Brooke. She stepped closer to Squeege. Right now even that giant seemed more comforting than the captain.

"Ofttimes we rue the things we do," Captain Blade said, wearily rubbing his neck. "And so God has seen fit to punish me by plaguing me with this brat. Keep an eye on her, will you, Squeege? If you have to chain her to your ankle, by heavens, do something with the girl!"

"Aren't we going to go back to England now?" Brooke asked, gathering her courage. "After all, you don't have a compass or maps."

The captain gave her a rueful smile. "Fortunately, miss, I still have my astrolabe and the stars. I could get us to Virginia by the stars alone if I had to, so don't be thinking about stealing my astrolabe. I thank God above that you can't steal the stars."

"What's an astrolabe?" Brooke asked, but Squeege turned her from the captain and prodded her toward the companionway.

"I'll see that she's safely put away," Squeege said, following Brooke. "If I have to, I'll put a barrel on the hatch. There's not a child down there that could lift a barrel."

79

"Something tells me an elephant couldn't stop that she-devil," the captain muttered as Brooke moved away. "Keep her out of my sight, Squeege."

8

S queege made a great to-do about returning
Brooke to the hold, and Kimberly and the others
had no idea what the ruckus was about until
Thatcher broke the news. "She said she was
going to steal the captain's maps so we couldn't get to
Virginia," he said, raking his hands through his dark hair
as his eyes gleamed with excitement. He turned toward
Brooke. "So tell us—were you able to do it?"

"I was," Brooke said, lifting her chin. "I crumpled up
all his maps and threw them out the window. And I threw
the compass overboard, too."

"You didn't!" Kimberly wailed. "What if we can't get
anywhere?" She covered her cheeks with her hands.
"Brooke, that was a stupid thing to do. Without his compass, the captain won't know where to go—"

"Don't worry," Brooke said, a frown settling onto
her pretty face. "Captain Blade said he could steer by the
stars if he had to. And he said he uses an astrolabe." She

glanced up at Thatcher with a hopeful expression. "What's an astrolabe?"

"You'll not be getting that from him," Thatcher answered. "He keeps it at his belt, he does. An astrolabe is a sailor's right hand."

Brooke shrugged. "Well, I'm not giving up. I'm not going to Virginia. I'll just have to think of something else to get the captain to turn this ship around."

"You won't be getting out through the hatch again," Wingate called. The other children looked at him, and he pointed up the staircase. "I just heard a noise from up there. Someone's moved something heavy over the door."

"When there's a will," Brooke muttered with dark promise, "there's a way. When I set my mind out to get something, I always get it."

"Captain Blade is not your papa," Kimberly said, her words more biting than she'd intended them to be. "He won't give in to your demands."

Brooke didn't answer but tossed her head and moved to sit in an empty corner.

* * *

Most of the children slept peacefully that night as the dark came on. Unable to sleep and worried about her mother's ragged breathing, Kimberly moved to the window to look out upon the world. Ahead of the ship, the sun submerged itself in the great ocean, leaving a copper-colored sheen on the water and a reddish glow in the western sky. A few moments later, the velvet darkness of night surrounded the ship, and the waves lifted to the stars as the *Seven Brothers* cut her way through the sea.

Someone stirred in the darkness beyond her, and as Kimberly's eyes adjusted to the dim light of the moon, she saw Ethan sitting not far away. "Have you said your kaddish?" she asked, tossing the question quietly over her shoulder.

82

"Nay," Ethan answered, his voice low and soothing. "I have been thinking about other things."

"Whether we'll get lost?"

"Nay. I trust the captain."

"What, then?

"*Baruch Dayan emet,*" Ethan whispered, and Kimberly remembered what the words meant: "Blessed is the Judge of Truth."

"*Baruch atah Adonai, Eloheinu melech ha-olam,*" Ethan went on, his voice strangely musical in the quiet of the ship. "Blessed are you, O Lord, our God, King of the universe." *King of the universe.* If God was King, she was his subject. If he was King, she ought to obey him without complaining. And because he was a loving God, she knew she ought to trust him without fear.

But it wouldn't be easy.

9

Kimberly sank to the floor and pulled her mother's head into her lap. Her mama was weaker today, and the scrap of blanket Thatcher had given her was bloody after she had coughed into it. Prickles of cold dread crawled along Kimberly's back when she saw the stained blanket. Her mother was sick enough to cough up blood! And yet she had still wanted to come on this voyage.

Her mother's forehead burned with fever, and at night her clothing and skin were damp with sweat. Kimberly didn't know what to do. There was no fresh water save that which they were given at mealtime; no soup, no soft bread, no blankets, no pillows. Nothing to ease her mother's discomfort. With every day Mistress Hollis had grown thinner, and bruises from lying on the hard floor were already beginning to show on her elbows and knees.

After making sure that her mother's eyes were closed, Kimberly leaned back against the timbers of the ship and covered her face with her hands. Tears filled her eyes as she gave way to the flood of emotions that threatened to drown her. What else could she do but cry?

A welcome breeze blew hot through the hold and dispelled some of the sour smell. She felt her heavy hair lift in the wind, and she held her dirty hands out to feel the healing warmth of the sun.

A hand touched her shoulder, and Kimberly whirled around. "Soft, I didn't mean to frighten you," Thatcher said. He had crept up behind her without a sound, and Kimberly realized that he must have been a very good pickpocket indeed.

"What do you want?" she asked, her voice a bit unsteady.

"Only this," Thatcher said, resting his elbows upon the windowsill. His dark eyes swept across the unending waters. "You ought to speak to the captain about your mother. Since most merchant ships don't have a doctor aboard, many times the captain himself knows a bit of medicine. He might be able to help her."

Kimberly chewed on her thumbnail. She hadn't thought of that, but Thatcher was probably right.

86

"Will you go with me?" she asked, her stomach churning at the thought of facing Captain Blade. "He seems so rough and cruel—"

"I'll stand right behind you," Thatcher promised. "Speak to him today at dinner. I wouldn't put it off another day."

* * *

At dinnertime the captive children were led down to the lower deck, and Kimberly did not hesitate to approach the captain. He stood with a group of grizzled seamen as he ate, but his eyes grew alert as he saw her come toward him.

"What is it, miss?" he asked, wiping his moustache on his sleeve. "Do you have a complaint?"

"Nay, sir," she said, gathering up her slippery courage. "'Tis my mother. She's not well, and one of the boys said you might be able to help her."

"I sent her to you, sir," Thatcher said, appearing suddenly at Kimberly's elbow. "I know men of the sea often have a knowledge of medicine."

The captain squinted in dark amusement. "I know how to bind up a sword wound and apply a poultice to a sting from a jellyfish," he said. "Has your mother one of those?"

"Nay," Kimberly answered, dismayed that he wasn't taking her seriously. "She coughs a lot, and lately she has been coughing up blood."

All traces of humor disappeared from the captain's eyes. He tossed his plate onto the serving table. "Where is your mother?" he asked, his voice quiet and intense.

Kimberly pointed upward. "Up in our hold. She hasn't the strength to come down the stairs."

The captain moved to the food line in three giant steps, pocketed a handful of biscuits from the barrel, then climbed the staircase. Before disappearing from sight, he called down to Kimberly, "Make sure y'eat, miss. I'll take care of your mother."

* * *

Kimberly felt a little better after the captain left, and she felt positively friendly toward Squeege when he helped her get a plate so she wouldn't have to stand in line. "We've seen this sickness before," Squeege said, handing Kimberly her tin of cold beef and sea biscuit. He led her to a row of barrels and she followed his example and perched on top of one to eat.

"Will she get better?" Kimberly asked, hoping for good news.

Squeege shook his head. "Only God knows," he said. "If y'are a praying person—"

"I am," Kimberly answered.

"Then pray for your mother. Mayhap God will give her the strength to see the journey through. But we're not even a week at sea, and we've many weeks more to go. The food begins to grow stale, the fresh water blackens—" Squeege stopped suddenly, as if he had just remembered to whom he spoke. "But I don't mean to worry your head with such things. You can trust the captain to get this ship safely to port."

"Where are we sailing, exactly?" Thatcher asked, coming over. He mumbled around a mouthful of the dry bread. "'Tis warmer here than in England."

"Aye," Squeege answered, grinning so widely that Kimberly could see the black teeth at the corners of his mouth. "Y'are right, me boy. We've sailed south toward the Canary Islands, which we'll see in a day or two, if we're lucky. Then we'll head west to catch the great winds that will send us to the New World. 'Tis a journey of six weeks at best, twelve at worst."

"Six weeks," Kimberly whispered. How could her mother live like this for another six weeks?

88

* * *

Mistress Hollis was awake when the children returned to their hold, and she smiled faintly at Kimberly as she sat up and sipped the mug of water the captain had brought her. "He's really a kind man," she whispered to Kimberly. "Gruff and tough, to be sure, but I think there's a good heart underneath that solid exterior. We must keep praying that he will change his mind about selling these poor captives."

"You should rest, Mama," Kimberly said, placing her hands on her mother's shoulders to force her back down.

"Nay," her mother answered, gently pushing Kimberly's hands away. "I'm done with resting for a while. I need to sit up and spend some time with all these children." She looked up at Kimberly, and a smile crinkled the corners of her eyes. "Isn't it strange? I always wanted more children, and now I have over a hundred, if even for a few weeks. God does work in mysterious ways his wonders to perform."

Several of the younger children, thrilled that Mistress Hollis was awake and talking, crept forward and seated themselves around her feet. Even Christian and Abigail moved closer, and Kimberly realized that the others were desperate for a mother's attention. So many of them had been orphaned before they came aboard the ship. And Brooke, who sat quietly in a corner, had a mother but never saw her.

An intriguing, unsettling thought entered Kimberly's mind: Though she had nothing in the world but the clothes she wore, she had a mother. None of the other children did. As she pondered the thought, the bitter gall of jealousy burned the back of her throat. What right did all these people have to *her* mother?

She stood and moved away as twin demons of jealousy and anger wrestled in her head. She wanted to be as kind and generous as she knew she ought to be, but within the last few days, Kimberly had left everything she had ever loved and now stood to lose even her mother to a group of sad, sorry children.

10

Brooke shifted uncomfortably on the hard floor and knocked her fist against her forehead, trying to think. With every hour, the ship sailed farther away from England. Her hunger strike hadn't worked and neither had stealing the captain's maps and compass. What would make the captain want to forget about selling his captives in Virginia?

She couldn't pretend to be sick, because Mistress Hollis's illness hadn't stopped the captain from pressing on. And none of the boys seemed likely to start a riot or rouse the sailors to mutiny—

Revolution. If she could stir up enough trouble in the passenger hold, maybe the captain would decide it would be easier to return them to England than continue with them for another two or three months. *'Twould be easy to stir things up,* she schemed.

Rising from her corner, Brooke smoothed her kirtle, twisted a stray curl around her finger, and smiled in contemplation of her plan. It was time to begin, and if all went well, this ship would be pointed toward England before sunset.

She walked to where Denni and Daryl sat together quietly. "Hello," she said. When Denni looked up, Brooke jumped and landed with both feet upon Denni's soft leather slippers.

Denni clutched her foot and screamed in pain. Daryl leapt to his feet with his fists clenched. He rattled off a furious question in French, and Brooke answered with a swift punch to his stomach. Daryl doubled over, gasping for breath, and suddenly every boy and girl in the room rose to face Brooke, their eyes either frightened or furious.

Wingate was one of the first to confront her. "Have you popped your cork?" he asked, striding bravely forward as if she wouldn't dare do anything to him. Brooke grabbed a handful of Wingate's brown hair and yanked on it as he howled in fury. Ethan ran to tug on Brooke's arm, determined to loose it from Wingate's scalp, and Christian shuffled forward, pawing the air until he reached the scuffling trio. He thrust his arms around Brooke's waist and held her as others ran to free Wingate and grab her arms before she could harm anyone else.

"Throw her overboard!" someone shouted. "The captain won't care!"

Brooke felt herself being lifted into the air. She gasped in fright. She had known her plan was risky, but things were definitely out of control now. At least thirty hands joined to carry her toward the open window, and the only pair of compassionate eyes Brooke could see belonged to Kimberly Hollis. "Help!" she managed to squeak.

Kimberly left her mother's side and rushed into the crowd to grab Brooke's feet. "Nay!" she said, tugging

92

Brooke back into the safety of the center of the ship. "You can't throw her out the window!"

"Why not?" Thatcher called from the edge of the crowd. Although he was not among the children lifting Brooke, he was clearly enjoying the spectacle. "She's a brat, and she's driving us crazy with her whining."

"You can't do this!" Kimberly insisted, still pulling on Brooke's feet. Brooke closed her eyes and screamed in earnest, feeling like the rope she'd seen children use as they played tug-of-war. From her corner Mistress Hollis protested in a weak voice, and Abigail and Christian suddenly grabbed Brooke's legs and helped Kimberly pull her away from the yawning empty space of the window. Brooke's hands, arms, and legs were securely imprisoned, and she could do nothing but scream as she was carried first one way, then the other, as the two groups of children battled for her life.

Several of the smaller youngsters began to howl in genuine fear at the sound and fury of the fight, and suddenly the trapdoor above flew open and Squeege's wide body filled the empty space. "What the devil is going on down here?" he roared, coming down the stairs. He waded into the crowd, tossing children out of his way, until he reached Brooke. At the sight of Squeege's big hands and broad back, the children dropped her and fled to the walls of the chamber. Choking back her sobs, Brooke sat up and opened her eyes. She sat alone with Squeege in the center of the hold.

"What's the reason for this?" Squeege asked, frowning as he looked around the room. "Why were ye about to offer this girl to the sharks?"

Brooke didn't give anyone else a chance to answer. "They hate me, and I demand to see the captain," she said, wiping tears from her face. This fight would still work to her advantage. If she could convince Captain Blade that this kind of fighting would go on every day, he might return to England. No grown-up could handle this kind of noise without eventually going crazy.

"You be quiet," Squeege answered, giving her a stern glance. He lifted his eyes and glanced around the room. "Now, who's going to tell me the cause of this ruckus?"

Several children offered explanations:

"We *do* hate her."

"She's a crybaby."

"She stomped on Denni's feet for no reason at all."

"And hit Daryl."

"And she's a snob. She thinks she's better than anyone else."

Squeege held up a hand for quiet and pressed his lips into a thin line. "I begin to see," he said, helping Brooke to her feet. "Well, I've got news for all of ye. Nobody tosses anybody overboard without the captain's permission. We'll take her up to Captain Blade and see what he thinks of this. Mayhap he'll make her swab the upper decks today."

"Nay," Brooke wailed, genuine sorrow filling her heart. "My hands!" She thrust her lower lip out in a pout. "You'll ruin my hands with mopping."

"Would you rather swim with the sharks?" Squeege asked, taking her arm.

Brooke bit her lip, then let him lead her up the stairs to face the captain.

* * *

Captain Blade had spread new parchments on the table in his cabin and was busy making notes. He barely even looked up from his work as Squeege explained the problem, and all Brooke could see of the captain was his long, dark hair and his plumed hat. "I'll have no fighting on my ship," he finally said, lifting his face to glance up at Brooke. "I won't allow it among my men, and I won't be having it among my cargo."

"Excuse me, sir," Brooke said, her cheeks burning. "But we are not cargo—we're passengers."

The corner of the captain's mouth lifted in a half smile. "Aye, so y'are. Well, little miss, I'll not take trouble or rebellion from my passengers, either. And since y'are the only one to cause me trouble thus far, you'll set the example for the others. Today you'll stand at the mizzen-mast from now until sunset, with no dinner and no water. And if I hear a peep out of you, I'll stuff a canvas rag into your mouth to keep you quiet."

"You can't!" Brooke gasped. "My skin! My nanny has taken such pains to keep it white, I'll get all burnt if I stand out in the sun."

The captain's eyes stirred to anger as he looked up at her, and Brooke realized that he wasn't kidding. Throughout the years her nanny, the cooks, and the butler had threatened her with punishments of one kind or another, but her father wouldn't have allowed them to actually do anything to her. But now her father wasn't here, and this man didn't care one whit about her.

She swallowed noisily and bit her lip to keep from crying. For the first time in her life, Brooke Burdon was *really* scared.

"I'm sorry," she managed to whisper. "I just thought that mayhap you'd take the ship back to England to get rid of me—"

"Young lady," Captain Blade answered, not looking up. "If I want to be rid of you, I'll confine you to the orlop deck or toss you into the deep. But I'm not about to let your ravings and temper interfere with this voyage. Do you understand?"

"Yea."

He looked up at her then, his eyes hard and penetrating. "I didn't hear you. I said, *do you understand?*"

"Yea, sir, Captain Blade," she answered, strengthening her voice.

"Good." The captain nodded to Squeege. "Lash her to the mizzenmast, and leave her there until the sun sets and the other children are quiet. Then you can return her below, but I do not want to see her face again in this cabin until we arrive in Virginia. Is that clear?"

Brooke thought that even Squeege looked a little frightened as he nodded in answer.

* * *

Brooke wasn't sure what was the worst part of her punishment—being forced to stand under the gaze of two dozen sailors who winked and teased her as they worked on the sails, or watching them all go downstairs to eat while her stomach knotted in hunger. And as the sun grew hot overhead and the shadows disappeared, she grew so thirsty that she would have drunk her own sweat if she could have caught it. She was surrounded by water as far as she could see, but she had not a drop to drink. Her tongue felt heavy and swollen in her mouth, and her head swam with dizziness.

The air rippled with heat as the seamen worked through the long afternoon and sang their sea chanties. As the sun dipped gradually in the west, Brooke felt her head fall upon her chest. Why did bad things always happen to her? Other spoiled rich girls lived on Eton Court, so why was she the only one kidnapped? And why was ordinary Kimberly Hollis a paying passenger while Brooke was merely cargo? Kimberly had her mother and friends, while Brooke had nothing. Suddenly part of her wished that Kimberly had let the others toss her out the window. Better to be alone in the sea than lonely on this ship where everyone from the captain to the lowest bilge boy hated her.

As the sunlight faded from the sky, the sailors hunkered down to talk and smoke their pipes. The deck was oddly quiet over the steady slush and splash of the water against the ship. Brooke felt a tear begin to roll down her cheek. She wanted to wipe it away so the seamen wouldn't know she'd been crying, but her hands were tied to the mizzenmast.

* * *

The squeak of the hatch woke Kimberly from a light sleep, and she opened one eye as Brooke climbed down the stairs in the dim light of early evening. The pretty blonde girl walked stiffly, and her face was red and puffy with sunburn. She sank onto an empty spot of floor and lay down without saying anything to anyone as the trapdoor lowered with a soft thud.

Kimberly lowered her head to her arm. She couldn't deny that Brooke had deserved some punishment, but still she felt sorry for the girl. Moving from a life of luxury to being a prisoner couldn't be easy.

She had just closed her eyes to sleep again when a hot, water-scented wind blew through the open windows. A hissing sound echoed through the ship. Alarmed, Kimberly sat up. Had they sailed into the nest of giant sea serpents? Her eyes scanned the gray space outside the windows, then she sighed in relief. A gentle silvery rain fell in the dim moonlight and thrummed gently on the roof overhead.

97

She lay back down. She was more nervous than she'd realized if a simple thing like rain could upset her. A moment later, Kimberly felt a cold drop fall on her forehead and slide into her hair. That drop was joined by others, and soon Kimberly felt as though she were sleeping outdoors. It would be a long night if this kept up.

"Kimberly." A hand fell upon her shoulder, and she sat up, startled.

"What? Who's there?"

"'Tis only me, Thatcher."

Kimberly relaxed as she recognized Thatcher's voice. "What's wrong?" she whispered. "Is aught amiss?"

"Nay," he said, and though she couldn't see his face in the dim light, she could hear a smile in his voice. "'Tis your mother. We shouldn't be letting her get wet like this."

"Welladay, what am I supposed to do?" Kimberly asked, a little annoyed. "I have no canopy for her head. 'Tis of certain raining harder than this on the deck above, and I won't take her to the decks below, not with rats in the food barrels—"

"'Tis drier in the stern," Thatcher said. He had moved to Mistress Hollis's side. "There's a deck above the stern, don't you remember? The stern is drier than this middle area. So, are you going to help me carry your mother and her things?"

"Yea."

Thatcher grunted softly as he lifted Mistress Hollis, and Kimberly put a hand on Thatcher's shoulder so he could lead her through the dark toward the back of the ship.

"Here," he said finally. Thatcher knelt and placed Kimberly's mother on the floor. There was no response from Mistress Hollis.

Kimberly sat down and put her head against her knees, fighting against despair. Her mother had been very quiet ever since Brooke was taken to the upper deck, and Kimberly didn't know if she was asleep or unconscious. While Thatcher sat with her, Kimberly could see his face in the gray light of the cloud-covered moon. His face was stained with weariness but seemed lighted from within, as if he'd enjoyed doing a good deed.

"Why'd you do this?" Kimberly asked, grateful for his help but not sure why he offered it.

Thatcher's eyes glistened like stars in the night. "I

had a mother—once," he whispered. His voice was husky. "I loved her."

"What happened to her?"

Thatcher shrugged and lifted his head toward the window. "She died. And then I wished I'd been nicer to her while she was alive."

Kimberly didn't say anything else, and after a few moments Thatcher stood and moved away toward the wet, empty space where Kimberly and her mother had been sleeping. Kimberly lay down to rest, but someone else moved in the darkness, so she lifted herself on one elbow to look around. In the dim light she saw Christian rise to his feet and tread lightly across the floor. "Excuse me," he whispered each time he brushed his foot against a sleeping child's body. "Pardon me."

His gray beggar's cup gleamed in his hand, and Kimberly lifted her head and watched with interest as he held it out the window to collect the precious fresh rainwater. *What a good idea*, she thought, smiling. When he was finished drinking, she'd ask to borrow his cup so her mother could have a drink. The water they were given at dinner was stale and smelled of the sour hold where the food was stored. Fresh rainwater would taste as if it had come from the wellsprings of heaven.

Christian steadily held his cup out, leaning precariously over the window's edge, until he had filled it. Kimberly watched as he brought it to his face, sniffed it appreciatively, then he continued shuffling across the floor. "Brooke?" he whispered, waking several children as he slowly progressed through the ship. "Where are you?"

"Here," Brooke croaked, lifting her head. Her golden hair shone in the dim light.

"I thought you'd need water," Christian said, lowering the cup to her.

Surprised beyond words, Kimberly watched as Christian, to whom Brooke had never offered a kind word, knelt and gave his enemy a drink. When Brooke had drunk most of the water, she handed the cup back to him, and Christian carefully dipped his fingers into the water, then wet Brooke's sunburned face. Brooke closed her eyes and accepted his help without comment.

Across the hold, Kimberly fumed. *She's so used to being spoiled she probably has no idea how nice Christian is,* she thought. *And why would Christian bring water to her when my mother needs it, Abigail needs it, Wingate needs it, I need it, even Christian himself needs it! And yet he takes water to the person who least deserves his help!*

Christian poured the rest of the water, only a few drops, onto Brooke's head, then she lay down in the darkness as he shuffled away. But he didn't go back to sleep. He stood again at the window, his cup outstretched as the rain fell.

If he takes Brooke Burdon another cup of water . . . , Kimberly thought, scowling. But he didn't. When the cup was full, Christian turned in the darkness and called out "Kimberly? Where is your mother?"

"Over here," she said, feeling a bit guilty for her harsh thoughts. Christian moved carefully toward her, and when he was close enough, Kimberly put her hand on his arm. "Aren't you scared to creep around at night?" she asked, taking the cup he offered.

"Is it nighttime?" A teasing smile flitted across his face. "I thought 'twas high noon."

Kimberly blushed. How foolish could she be? Day and night were alike to a blind boy. Christian was probably the one person aboard ship who could have moved around in the darkness without spilling every drop of the precious rainwater. She held the cup to her mother's dry lips and sighed in relief when her mother weakly took a sip. When she had finished drinking, Kimberly used the rest of the cupful to wash her mother's face and hands.

"Thank you, Christian," Kimberly whispered, noticing that the sound of rain had lessened. She placed the small cup in his hand. "I hope you'll be able to get another cupful for yourself."

"I don't need it," Christian answered, moving steadily away. "But there are others who do."

Wrapped in a warm bundle of gratitude, Kimberly stretched out on the wet floor and closed her eyes, willing herself to sleep.

* * *

Brooke choked back angry tears as she lay on the cold floor. Despite the water that blind boy had brought her, her tongue still felt heavy and fuzzy, and her face and hands were burning from the touch of the sun. Why did her nanny ever bother to dress her in bonnets and gloves and long sleeves? A lifetime of pampering had been spoiled in one afternoon!

But Brooke had to admit she'd been caught in a web of her own weaving. She had done frightfully bad things, and Captain Blade was probably right to punish her. But how much easier it'd be if he'd just send her home! Couldn't he put her on one of those little boats and send her home with one of the sailors? She didn't want to go to America, and she didn't want to become someone's servant. She was Brooke Elizabeth Burdon, daughter of Sir Howard Henry Burdon and Lady Eleanor Lizette Mary Burdon of Eton Court.

At the thought of her parents, tears began to roll down her face and into her hair. Sir Howard and Lady Eleanor were her parents, in truth, but they were rarely home when she was. Never had her mother told her stories. Never had her father promised swift and unfailing discipline for the many times she'd burned her clothes, frazzled her nannies, and screamed at the cooks.

The soft rainfall stopped its steady tapping against the wooden planks over her head, and Brooke sniffed in relief. Now mayhap she'd be able to go to sleep. She was cold, soaked, and as miserable as she'd ever been in her life. She wanted to close her eyes and forget that any of this had ever happened. Perhaps she'd wake up in her own bed at home. Perhaps this had all been a terrible nightmare, a horrible dream.

But as she covered her ears to block the soft breaths and occasional nighttime cries of the other children, Brooke knew that her situation was real. What would it take for God to forgive her so she could go home and try to be good? *When Mistress Hollis wakes up*, Brooke thought, *I'll ask her.*

Sunday, May 16

11

When sunrise painted the sky with the colors of a new day, Kimberly stirred from her place and looked at her mother. Mistress Hollis was pale and her skin seemed almost transparent, but ragged breaths came from her parted lips. Kimberly thanked God that her mother had lived through the damp coolness of the rainy night.

The other children stirred gradually, and several laughed as they stretched and began to move about. Everyone and everything in the cabin had been coated with a fine layer of salt from the sea air. When combined with the dampness of the rain, the salt stiffened the children's hair, clothing, and shoes.

"Methinks I could take off this shirt and have it walk up alone to say good morrow to the captain," Wingate joked, coming over to sit with Kimberly. He jerked his head toward her sleeping mother. "How's your mama?"

"Fine," Kimberly answered, giving her friend a

smile. "Thatcher told me about this spot last night. He gave it up himself so my mother could have a dry place to sleep."

"Drier, you mean," Wingate corrected, looking pointedly at Mistress Hollis's wet clothes.

Christian abruptly lifted his head and sniffed the air. "What's up?" Kimberly called, joking. "Don't tell me you smell roast beef for dinner."

"Nay," Christian said, his face serious. "There's a change in the air."

"Can you tell the future?" Thatcher called.

"Not that kind of change," Christian said. "'Tis the weather."

"Y'are a bit late," Brooke called from her place, her voice flat. "The rain came last night, or don't you remember that?"

"I remember," Christian said, but his face remained troubled.

Ethan looked out the window. "The sky's nothing but blue," he announced, turning back to the others. "Not a cloud in sight."

"Mayhap I'm wrong," Christian said, his wide eyes seeing nothing. "But I sense something."

104   Kimberly frowned, but Thatcher gave her a confident smile. "Don't let it worry you," he said, helping her spread out the wet clothing of several of the younger children. "'Tis clear and beautiful on both sides of the ship."

"Kimberly?" The quiet murmur cut through the hubbub of children's voices, and the older children turned toward the spot where Mistress Hollis lay.

"How are you, Mama?" Kimberly asked, hurrying to her mother's side.

"All right," her mother answered, giving her a smile. "Will you help me sit up, dear? Mayhap I could lean against the wall."

Kimberly and Thatcher worked together to lift

Mistress Hollis into a sitting position. When she was settled comfortably, she gave them both a smile. "Such a pretty day," she said, her eyes falling on the blue spaces behind the open windows. "They say that the skies are usually clear in Virginia, not cloudy like they are in England."

"Soft, Mama, you shouldn't talk so much," Kimberly said, pushing a strand of wet hair from her mother's eyes. "You'll set yourself to coughing."

"I feel quite rested," her mother answered, taking a shallow breath. "I am quite happy to know that I'll be seeing your father very soon."

"Rest, Mama," Kimberly urged, tucking her mother's wet kirtle around her ankles. "We'll talk about Papa later."

* * *

From across the cabin Brooke was glad to see Mistress Hollis awake and sitting up. She had questions to ask, and she couldn't spend another sleepless night worrying about whether or not God would hate her forever. As soon as Kimberly had left her mother's side to help the younger children take off their wet clothes, Brooke stood up and hurried to the stern of the ship.

"Good morrow, Mistress Hollis," she said politely, kneeling at the woman's feet. "I hope you slept well."

Mistress Hollis's smile sparkled like a garden after a spring rain. How could she be so happy after such a horrid night?

"I did rest well, Brooke," the woman answered. "Did you?"

"Well, nay," Brooke said, fidgeting with her hands in her lap. "I kept thinking about God and punishment. And—well, I think I may have been a wee bit snappish. And mayhap that's why the captain tied me up yesterday until I was thirsty and sunburned."

105

"'Tis not for me to judge your heart," Mistress Hollis answered with a little cough. "'Tis for you to judge your own. But I can tell you that the Bible says pride goeth before a fall. Have you taken a fall, dear Brooke?"

"Oh, yea," Brooke answered. "A mighty fall. So how can I *change?* I am cursed to be a captive on this ship—"

"Oh, my dear," Mistress Hollis said, her voice quiet and full of sympathy, "I do not believe that you are cursed. This is an unfortunate situation, but our God is strong enough to make good come out of bad. Remember the story of the prophet Daniel? He, too, was kidnapped. He was stolen from his home and parents to serve in a foreign king's court. And Joseph was a captive, sold into slavery in a foreign land—"

"Just like me?" Brooke asked, gasping.

"Yea," Mistress Hollis answered. "Just like you. But God worked in and through each of those young boys, and he can work through you, too, if you'll allow him to have his way." She placed her pale hand upon Brooke's flaming cheek. "Your words do not have to be snappish, dear Brooke. You can speak with words of pure gold if you will allow God to control your tongue."

"But how do I do that?" Brooke cried.

Mistress Hollis smiled. "Happy are the poor in spirit, for theirs is the kingdom of heaven," she whispered. "Our Lord Jesus said you will be happy, Brooke, when you think of yourself as a servant, not a pampered princess. When you decide to become a lowly servant of our Lord and Savior, you'll begin to adjust your ways. What you *do* reflects who you *are.*"

Who was she? Brooke pondered the question. She was the daughter of Sir Howard Henry Burdon and Lady Eleanor Lizette Mary Burdon of Eton Court—or at least she had been. Now she was a captive bound for the colonies, just like the others in this ship. She couldn't depend on her parents, on the captain, on Squeege, on anyone but God.

Could she try to be Jesus' servant? That would mean giving up her plans to turn the ship back for England. It might mean becoming a field hand on a tobacco plantation.

She twisted the fabric of her kirtle, thinking. Though she couldn't guess what the future might hold, she knew for certain that she didn't want to be the spoiled, selfish, friendless girl who lived with a battalion of cooks and nannies at Eton Court. She wanted to be like Kimberly Hollis, a girl who made friends with everyone and who had a mother who loved her. If being a servant of Christ would make her more lovable . . .

"I'll try," she said, her eyes focused on Mistress Hollis. "I'll try to be God's servant."

Suddenly, in a breathless instant of release, she felt free. This was the beginning of a new identity, a new Brooke Burdon.

Smiling shyly, Brooke lowered her head toward Mistress Hollis's shoulder. She was almost afraid to actually touch the frail woman, but the lady drew Brooke's golden head down into her lap and began to stroke her mussed hair. With every stroke Brooke felt her hard heart softening.

"If you have truly surrendered your pride this day," Mistress Hollis said, her voice warm and tender, "you must show Christ's love to the others here. Think of others first, Brooke, then of yourself. And when your old self rises to challenge your new heart, be strong in your faith that Jesus has changed you."

"I will," Brooke whispered, loving the woman's tender touch.

* * *

Kimberly stiffened when she saw Brooke's head in her mother's lap. For an instant the old serpent of jealousy

107

hissed in her heart, but then her mother lifted her gaze to meet Kimberly's, and Kimberly saw the light of joy in her mother's eyes. Something had happened! Kimberly moved closer in time to overhear that Brooke had surrendered her pride to God.

"You haven't been alone in feeling selfish," Kimberly said, sinking to the floor next to Brooke. She placed her hand on the girl's shoulder. "I'm not always what I ought to be, either."

"None of us is," her mother said gently. Kimberly noticed that her mother's eyelids seemed heavy. "That's why I pray for you, and why you must pray for each other."

Mistress Hollis rested a hand on each of the girls' heads and closed her eyes in prayer. "My dear heavenly Father," she prayed, her voice a golden ripple through the quiet of the hold. "I pray for these two children, and all the children of this ship. Keep them strong and safe until they reach Virginia. And keep their souls in your care, so they may know the joy that comes from serving you and serving others. Bless our captain and his men, and bless the bilge boys below who feed our bodies. But feed our souls, Lord, and make us to be what you want us to be. Amen."

Kimberly looked at her mother's loving face, but then a loud sniff caught her attention. Thatcher stood nearby, thumbing tears from his eyes.

12

Look out below! The wind freshens!" The sailor's cry echoed through the ship's creaking timbers, and Kimberly lifted her face toward the window. The sky had darkened during her talk with her mother, and a pillaring mass of steel gray thunderclouds seemed to be moving across the water straight toward them.

"Does a storm approach?" her mother asked, lying down in the small alcove at the stern of the ship.

"Yea," Kimberly answered quickly. "But you always did say you slept better in the rain."

"I do," her mother answered, her eyes closing slowly. "I'll sleep well. And I'll meet you and your father very soon, Kimmie."

"What?" Kimberly asked, confused, but her mother breathed deeply and did not answer. Kimberly turned again toward the window. Her mother spoke in riddles because she was not well, but there was a more pressing matter at hand—the storm.

Though it was early morning, the light in the hold dimmed, and the air in the chamber seemed to thicken around the children. Kimberly could hear the pounding of the sailors' feet overhead as they rushed to take in the sails, lest the ship be blown out of control by the suddenly strong winds. She turned again to check on her mother, but the lady still slept, her hand curled limply by her cheek. If God was merciful, Kimberly thought, she'd sleep through the entire storm.

"I'm scared," Brooke whispered, her eyes brilliantly blue in the darkness. "What's happening, Kimberly?"

"'Tis naught but a storm," Kimberly answered, her voice stronger than she felt. The ship began to pitch in a wild dance upon the water, and Kimberly clutched her stomach and shivered through a moment of fleeting nausea. She couldn't get sick now. She could feel the eyes of the other children upon her. They expected her to be an example.

Instinctively, she turned to Thatcher. His body was as rigid as a rock, his fists clenched at his side. "Tell them 'tis nothing to worry about," she called above the rising noise of the wind and sea. "Tell them that ships ride out storms like this every day."

110 "You can tell them," Thatcher barked in reply, and Kimberly bit her lip in frustration. She had hoped he'd be their leader now that her mother had fallen asleep, and yet he refused to do anything!

The hold quickly darkened, and the frightened cries of the other children quieted into gentle weeping and soft prayers. "Lord, have mercy upon us," Kimberly heard Brooke say. She looked at the other girl in amazement. There was nothing of the proud, spoiled daughter of Eton Court about Brooke now, and Kimberly rose to her knees to pray with the others. As their prayers rose to God's throne, Kimberly prayed that the stout wooden timbers of the ship would be strong enough to protect them from the furious, pounding waves outside. For a moment she felt as if she were entombed in a large coffin, soon to be buried in the depths of the sea. Surely it would only take one huge wave to sink the ship. One monstrous swell could take them all to the bottom of the deep.

Thunder crashed overhead, cracking like a whip through the hushed prayers around her. The *Seven Brothers* shuddered as rain poured down on their heads through cracks in the upper deck. The ship lifted and fell, rocked and listed; backward and forward, left and right. Not one of the children could stand. Even those who had been devoutly praying on their knees now lay flat on the floor, their bodies piled upon one another like an odd assortment of rag dolls. The air was horribly thick and close, and Kimberly threw herself on the floor next to Brooke and struggled to breathe a prayer: *God in heaven, have you abandoned us?*

Suddenly the ship began to roll from side to side as if a giant were playing with it. The boat listed right, and then left, and each time Kimberly stared at the wide windows as children's bodies tumbled closer and closer to the windowsill and the dark, churning waters. Brooke recognized the danger, too.

"What can we do?" Brooke yelled, pointing to the windows as the storm sent her crashing into Kimberly's shoulder. Kimberly threw her arms around Brooke, and together they slid across the deck and into the wall.

"Tell the others to go to the stern or the bow," Kimberly said, motioning toward the children in the midst of the cabin. "'Tis not safe in the center!"

The ship righted itself, and Brooke crawled off to warn the youngsters who were in the middle of the cabin. Kimberly felt a crazy smile cross her face when she looked up to see Christian clutching the mainmast in the very center of the cabin. He was singing, but she couldn't hear the song over the noise of the storm. Rain thrummed on the upper deck and sloshed in the ship's belly. The vessel thrashed amid the crack and roll of thunder.

Kimberly followed Brooke and reached another knot of children in the center of the cabin. She sent them to the bow as Brooke herded youngsters into the small, sheltered area at the stern. As a flash of lightning illuminated the hold, Kimberly looked up and saw a sight that horrified her—an army of roaches, disturbed by the churning waters in the belly of the ship, covered the walls like a glistening black blanket as they crawled upward in search of a dry resting place.

Kimberly shuddered and wiped her wet hair from her eyes to make sure no children were left in the unprotected center of the ship. Brooke had led Christian to safety in the stern, but in another white flash of lightening, Kimberly saw two huddled forms in the shadow of the mainmast. *Daryl and Denni!* The twins huddled there, wet and miserable, and if they weren't careful, they'd be carried out the window together.

Kimberly crawled on her hands and knees as she prayed the storm would calm long enough for her to bring the children to the others. "You must come with me," she shouted over the noise. The twins, wide-eyed with fear, only shook their heads and clung to each other more tightly.

Kimberly grabbed Daryl's shirt and pulled with all her might. "Come!" she shouted again, wishing that she knew even a few words of French.

"*Attendez une minute!*" Daryl screamed, his arms reaching out for his sister. Sobbing, Denni reached out for him, and Kimberly began to drag the unwilling pair to the stern. The ship tilted suddenly to the left, and a rogue wave washed through the open window. Salt water filled Kimberly's eyes and mouth and ears, and she lost her grip on Daryl's shirt. The ship tilted again, and the water rushed toward the openings on the other side of the ship, but Kimberly's fingers closed only on air.

"Daryl!" she screamed, blinking to focus her stinging eyes. "Denni!"

The screams of over a hundred children rent the air, but then a little voice seemed to speak directly to Kimberly's ear, *"Il fait froid,"* she heard a girlish whisper. Kimberly sighed in relief. The wave had washed Denni and Daryl behind her, and it would be a simple matter now to herd them into the larger group.

Her hands were raw and splintered by the time she had guided all of the children to a place of safety. As the ship continued to roll from side to side, she had the children lock hands and cling to each other.

For one eerie moment, the ship shifted to an even keel and the frightened whimpers around Kimberly eased. The hold seemed to grow brighter and the air still. Like the drawing of a breath, the storm quieted, the howling wind paused, the standing water on the deck floor shimmered in an unearthly gray light. Then lightning flashed, thunder cracked, and a fresh onslaught of rain slammed onto the deck above their heads. It was the most horrific and powerful noise Kimberly had ever heard, and the ship shivered under the sound.

113

"God help us!" Kimberly felt the cry escape her lips, and her arms reached to those around her as the ship rolled in the sea. The vessel twisted and fell against a wall of water that spewed forth from the openings above and broadside, but the chain of children held tight throughout the afternoon and into the night.

13

When the sun rose the next morning, Kimberly found it hard to believe that only a few hours earlier they'd nearly lost their lives to the sea. May laid a warm shoulder of sun against the ship to dry out the children's clothes, and the young ones forgot their modesty and stripped down to their petticoats and chemises to air their soaked laundry in the sun.

Kimberly breathed in a few deep gulps of fresh air at the window, then turned to the musty alcove where her mother waited. Her mother had slept through the rough night without coughing once, and surely she was better this morning. Probably hungry, too, Kimberly realized as her own stomach growled. Yesterday the storm had demanded all their attention; no one had eaten anything. Everyone would be thankful for the ship's biscuits today.

"Mama?" She crawled over to the low space where her mother lay on her side, her arm thrown across her chest as if she were reaching for something. "Mama, are you awake?"

Kimberly gently shook her mother's shoulder. Mistress Hollis's eyes were closed, her hands cold, and her skin an unnatural gray blue. Kimberly shook her again, realizing for the first time that something was very wrong. "Mama!" she called, only half aware that her voice had risen to a shriek. "Mama? Wake up! You must wake up! We didn't eat yesterday, you know, and I'm sure y'are hungry—"

She felt someone grab her shoulders and pull her away. Wingate spoke in her ear. "She's gone, Kimberly. Thatcher's fetching the captain now."

"Nay!" Kimberly broke free and knelt at her mother's side. "Mama!" she cried, afraid to touch her mother but wanting to bury her head in her mother's lap. "You can't leave me now! We have to meet Papa!"

She didn't know how long she sat there talking to her mother, but strong arms raised her from the floor, and Squeege led her from the stern of the ship while two seamen and Captain Blade carried her mother's body from the small alcove. Squeege stood by the window and asked Kimberly to watch the waves.

116   "Believe you in God?" Squeege asked, his eyes on the watery horizon.

"Yea," Kimberly answered, her voice a despairing whisper.

"Then you shall see her again," Squeege answered. "Do not fret, girl. In time you will grow accustomed to death. I have buried many a man in the sea."

But I want my mother! Kimberly wanted to cry out. But she said nothing, and after a while Squeege awkwardly patted her on the shoulder and left the hold. She went back to the alcove and sat cross-legged on the floor, cocking her head as if she could hear her mother's voice in the wind that whistled over the waters. "*I'll meet you and your father very soon, Kimmie,"* her mother had said. Had she known she would die?

There were no answers in the quiet after the storm, and Kimberly hung her head as tears fell down her cheeks like rain.

* * *

"She's over there, Captain." Thatcher's voice seemed to come from far away, and Kimberly flinched when a large hand fell upon her shoulder. "Miss Hollis?" The captain's voice cut through her thoughts. "We'll be burying your mother in a few moments. I thought you might want to come up for the service."

Kimberly felt a rock fall through her heart at the captain's words. "Can't we take her to Virginia? She wanted to go to Virginia, Captain. She wanted to see my father."

The captain's dark eyes clouded with understanding and pity. "Nay, child, we must bury her. I'm thinking she'd approve." His hand reached down and took Kimberly's, and she let him lead her toward the companionway to the upper deck. Before he allowed her to climb up, the captain paused. "Be there any of these children you'd like to stand with you?"

Kimberly looked around at the group. It seemed that a hundred pairs of sad eyes studied her, each face more forlorn than the next. "Abigail," she said, pointing to the girl. "And Thatcher, Ethan, Christian, and Wingate. And Brooke, if she wants to come."

"I'll come," Brooke said, stepping carefully through the children huddled before her. Ethan, Abigail, Christian, Thatcher, and Wingate followed Brooke, and Kimberly led the way up the stairs.

A fresh breeze ruffled her hair as she stepped out onto the deck. Honey-thick sunshine bathed the rigging and masts of the ship. The captain's crew stood in a single line at the rail around the ship's deck, and they bowed their heads in respect as Kimberly passed by. Wrapped in a beautiful red cloak, her mother's thin body lay on the deck near the mainmast.

"Oh," Kimberly caught her breath, moving closer. She'd never seen a cloak as thick and lovely. "This wasn't my mother's. We could never afford anything this nice—"

"'Twas my wife's," the captain said behind her, his voice heavy with emotion. "She has been gone now for five years." He paused, and Kimberly had to strain to hear his next words: "I still miss her terribly."

Kimberly folded her hands and smiled her thanks at the captain. He didn't have to sacrifice his wife's things for her mother, but she was glad he had. The lovely red cloak disguised how thin and drawn her mother had become. In it she looked peaceful, as if she were only sleeping.

The captain opened a *Book of Common Prayer* and began to read the burial service. Kimberly felt Brooke tug on her sleeve, so she turned from the sight of her mother and looked at the captain while the seamen stood in silent respect.

"We therefore commit her body to the deep," the captain read, glancing only occasionally at the small book in his hand. "To be turned into corruption, looking for the resurrection of the body and the life of the world to come through our Lord Jesus Christ. At his coming he shall change our vile bodies so that they may be like his glorious body, according to the mighty working whereby he is able to subdue all things to himself."

The sailors and children on deck lifted their heads at the conclusion of the prayer, but Kimberly did not feel comforted. Her mother never used such big and flowery words. That wasn't the kind of service her mother would want.

"Wait, I beg you," Kimberly called in a loud voice. She stepped away from Brooke and the other children and stood alone in the center of the ship. "I'd like to pray for my mother, if I may."

Captain Blade nodded, giving permission.

Kimberly bowed her head. Her heart overflowed with emotions she couldn't express, but she opened her mouth and hoped that she wouldn't cry. "My loving heavenly Father," she said, remembering the many times she'd heard her mother use that phrase, "I thank you that my mama lives with you this very minute. I thank you that she is no longer coughing or sick. But, dear God, I am here, and I'm alone, and I would ask you to comfort me. Help me learn how to live without a mother. . . ."

She stopped, unable to go on, but then an arm fell about her shoulders. "Help us all," Brooke prayed, her clear voice rising above Kimberly's sadness. "Mistress Hollis was a mother to all of us, and a teacher. So help us to know what we should be. Amen."

After Brooke's prayer Christian began to sing a hymn. A splash sounded during the song, but Kimberly did not turn toward the place where her mother had lain. Mistress Mary Hollis was no longer of this earth, but a citizen of the kingdom of God.

* * *

119

Kimberly accepted hugs of condolence from Brooke, Abigail, Ethan, Thatcher, Wingate, and Christian. She was about to follow them back down to the hold when Captain Blade tapped her on the arm. "I would have a moment of your time, Miss Hollis," he said, his dark eyes searching her face. He waited until the others had gone below; then he pointed up into the clear blue sky. "What see you there?"

Kimberly looked up. The sky was a wide blue bowl stretching without interruption or cloud as far as she could see. A flock of seagulls pinwheeled above the deck, calling noisily, but there was nothing unusual on the horizon.

"I see nothing," she said, turning again to the captain.

Captain Blade pointed to the birds overhead. "Gulls," he said, leaning on the ship's rail. "You will only see gulls where land is within two days' journey."

"Land?" Despite her sorrow, Kimberly felt her pulse quicken. Were they so close to Virginia?

"The Azores," the captain answered. "A group of islands owned by Portugal. The storm blew us off course, but God has had his hand in this, for many of our water barrels were cracked and spilt in the hold below. We will stop at the islands for fresh water."

The captain looked at her with a question on his face, and Kimberly stared back, confused. Why would he make a point of telling her about their water?

"Since you and your mother paid for your passage," the captain went on, his voice a shade softer, "I thought you might want to depart our ship in the Azores. If you wish, I could arrange passage for you on a ship back to England. I know not if you have friends or family still there, but since your mother has gone to God, I thought you might wish to return."

120

Return to England? A feeling of happiness rose inside Kimberly. She could go back and forget all this had ever happened! Master and Mistress Walker would be happy to take her in. She could work in the pie shop and make deliveries through the streets of London. She could feast her eyes on familiar sights instead of this watery wasteland. She could sleep again with Gretchen curled upon her chest and hear her cozy purring. . . .

But her mother had wanted her to go to Virginia. And her father waited for her in Jamestown.

"Can I think about my choice?" Kimberly asked the captain.

He nodded and pointed again to the birds. "We will be at the islands within two days," he said, nodding toward her. "Be sure you have made up your mind by the time we dock."

* * *

Kimberly ignored the compassionate glances of her fellow travelers and paced back and forth before the open windows of the hold. England seemed now to be a very dear and comfortable place, with jolly crowds of pedestrians clogging streets tight with the shops of merchants and the homes of the wealthy. Closing her eyes, she imagined the city as it had looked when she and her mother hurried home from the bakery at sunset. Lamps from the passing windows had pushed at the encroaching darkness, slanting yellow rectangles of light on the gray streets. Many-fingered swirls of dark smoke puffed up into the night sky from a thousand stoves and cozy hearth fires. Men and women tended their children and tucked them into comfy beds with dry sheets and creaky straw mattresses.

And the smells! The pie shop had smelled of yeast and meat and honey and sunshine even on the darkest, gloomiest days, and Mistress Walker always had the clean smell of soap about her. What Kimberly would give for a lump of soap now! She'd gone five days without clean water to wash her hair, her face, or her hands, and the ship's floor upon which she sat, walked, and slept was positively slimy beneath her feet. Things would only grow worse if she continued on to Virginia—the sour stench of wetness and rot would be overpowering after weeks aboard this ship.

Of course, if she left the *Seven Brothers* she'd have to endure another voyage back to England, and she'd likely be alone or under the protection of another traveler, possibly a stranger. There was danger in that, Kimberly knew, but surely Captain Blade wouldn't hand her over to

121

anyone who'd hurt her. And when the ship arrived in London, she'd get off at the docks and walk straight toward the Walkers' pie shop. 'Twould be a walk of an hour, maybe a little longer. When she reached her destination, she'd lean in the window, spy Mistress Walker, and call, "Hello! Guess who has come back to work for you!" And Mistress Walker would scream in delight and press her floury hands on Kimberly's cheeks. They'd embrace, and the lady would demand to know of Kimberly's mother, and so the story would be told. And then Mistress Walker would weep, and hug Kimberly again, and promise that Kimberly could live with them in the small attic room. She'd sleep that night in a proper bed. She'd wear a clean, decent nightgown, and Gretchen would rub against her legs, unable to believe that her girl had truly come home.

"I can't stand this a minute more." A sharp whine broke through Kimberly's pleasant vision, and she turned abruptly to stare at Brooke. The younger girl stood behind Kimberly in a small patch of sunlight cast through the open window, her face screwed up in a pout.

"What can't you stand?" Kimberly snapped, thinking that Brooke had no right to complain about anything. *She* hadn't just lost her mother.

122

"This wet!" Brooke said, spreading out her damp kirtle. "I've been standing in the sun here for ten minutes, and this fabric just won't dry. I told my nanny that we should use cambric instead of this damask, but she wouldn't listen—"

"Beshrew your nanny!" Kimberly shouted, feeling her cheeks burn as her temper flared. Every conversation in the hold stopped as children turned to stare at her. Ignoring them, she shook her finger in Brooke's face. "I don't care about your nanny! I don't care about anything right now, especially not your fancy dress! I'll go crazy if I have to listen to you one more day, Brooke Burdon!"

* * *

Brooke stood as stiff as a post, her arms hanging rigid at her sides, while Kimberly ranted and stormed around the hold. When Kimberly had finished all she wanted to say, she stomped off toward the small recess at the stern of the ship. Brooke hung her head as tears stung her eyes. Why was she always saying and doing the wrong thing? She hadn't meant to aggravate Kimberly, and she really didn't mean to imply that her clothes were better than anyone else's. She thought she was only making harmless conversation, for everyone knew that cambric was lighter than damask.

What had Mistress Hollis told her? *"When your old self rises to challenge your new heart, be strong in your faith that Jesus has changed you."*

She was Christ's servant now, and she needed to learn to think before speaking. Her dress was the finest aboard ship, and as she looked around at the rough fabrics of the other children's clothes, she realized that she should be grateful for what she had.

Guilt avalanched over her, pressing Brooke down with its weight. "I'm sorry," she whispered to the small group of children who watched her. "I'm so terribly sorry." Brooke saw Abigail's eyes soften, and she knew this time she'd said the right thing. But there were other, more important things yet to be done.

Brooke turned and walked to the back of the ship. Kimberly sat in the place where her mother had lain, hugging her knees to her chest.

"Kimberly, I didn't mean to upset you, and I'm sorry I did," Brooke said, sinking to the floor at Kimberly's side. "I guess I've always been a whiner. Old habits are hard to break, you know."

"I know," Kimberly answered. "I keep looking over here to check on my mother."

123

"I'm sorry," Brooke whispered, not knowing what else to say. "But will you be patient with me?"

"I don't know." Kimberly put her head down upon her knees, hiding her face from Brooke.

* * *

Kimberly wished Brooke would just go away. First she whined; then she came over to bother Kimberly again with a fake apology. Now she was asking Kimberly to be patient with her, when Kimberly had been nothing but patient for almost an entire week. How long was it going to take snotty Brooke to learn what even the poorest children on this ship already knew? *They* knew enough to be grateful for what they were given. *They* knew better than to bother a girl who had just lost her mother.

Brooke kept on talking in her thin, nasal voice, and though she wasn't listening to the words, Kimberly finally lost her patience. "Shut your mouth!" she cried, raising her head and clapping her hands over her ears. "Didn't you listen to a single thing my mother taught you? Didn't you mean anything you said when you were talking to my mother? Go away and be quiet!"

Brooke flushed to the roots of her golden hair as Kimberly yelled, and a look of honest hurt appeared in her eyes. Whimpering, Brooke clumsily rose to her feet and ran across the room, her hand over her mouth. A twinge of guilt struck Kimberly as she saw the girl sink into a frightened huddle on the opposite side of the ship, but the guilt was soon replaced by a feeling of triumph. She'd finally gotten rid of Brooke! And at dinner today she'd tell the captain that she wanted to return to England. And though Brooke had done nothing but whine about returning to England ever since she came aboard this ship, it would be Kimberly going home, not Brooke Burdon.

A gentle noise broke into her thoughts, and Kim-

124

berly looked up to see Wingate standing beside her. "What?" she asked crossly, not wanting him to spoil her moment of victory. He had probably come over to nag her, too.

"I heard what you said to Brooke," he said, his voice low and quiet. "And I think someone ought to say the same thing to you—after all, your mother would, if she were here."

"She would say *what?*" Kimberly asked, her head snapping toward him.

"Didn't you listen?" Wingate asked, mimicking her own voice. "Didn't you mean what you said?"

"What?" Kimberly shook her head in confusion.

"Happy are the poor in spirit, for theirs is the kingdom of heaven," Wingate whispered, and Kimberly remembered the words. *"Happy are you when you think of yourself as a servant. When you decide to become a lowly servant of our Lord and Savior, you'll begin to adjust your ways. What you* do *reflects who you* are."

"I've been a Christian since I was young," Kimberly said, rising to her feet to escape Wingate. "I'm not the one who's a brat. And I don't have to put up with this any longer."

125

She bolted from her place and hurried toward the companionway leading to the upper deck. She couldn't wait to tell the captain about her plans to leave the ship. She wasn't going to stay on this boat for one day longer than she had to.

* * *

The trapdoor leading to the upper deck was not blocked, and Kimberly easily pushed it open. It crashed onto the deck behind her, and before a sailor had time to come and investigate the noise, she was out of the hold and on her way to the captain's cabin.

"I'm here to see the captain," she called to Squeege,

who thrust his bearded face into her path as she stalked forward. "He'll know why I want to see him."

She knocked on the door and heard Captain Blade call, "Enter." When she pushed the door open, she saw him sitting at his desk, a stack of parchments before him. The captain was writing letters.

"Miss Hollis," he said, putting his pen down on his desk. He tented his fingers as his dark eyes widened in curiosity. "Have you made a decision?"

"I have," she said, thrusting her hands behind her back. She *had* made a decision to leave, but now that she stood in front of the captain her decision didn't feel right. The echo of her mother's voice ruffled through her mind like wind over the ocean waters: *"I would not have you be distressed, for I am taking you to your father. . . . God is calling us to America in faith, and we have taken the first step. . . . Promise me that you won't talk again about returning to England. For better or worse, we're bound for Virginia, and our lives are in God's hands."*

She had promised. Her mother had sold and lost everything she owned to put Kimberly aboard this ship, and Kimberly would be ignoring that great sacrifice if she returned to England now. Her mother would have died aboard this sour, rough ship for nothing.

"I will go on to America," Kimberly whispered, scarcely believing that her tongue could utter those words. A voice in her head screamed in protest, but her heart knew she had decided rightly.

The captain lifted an eyebrow in pleased surprise. "I see," he said, his tone indicating that he did not understand at all.

"There's only one thing," Kimberly said timidly, again thrusting her hands behind her back.

"What's that?" the captain asked, frowning.

"I won't be like them, will I?" she asked.

"Like who?"

126

"The captives. You won't sell me when we get to Jamestown?"

The captain laughed, and for a moment his dark face looked almost handsome. "I won't sell you, Miss Hollis. As I said, you and your mother were paying passengers. Your debt has already been paid."

She should have left the cabin then, but a spark of hope lit her soul. If the captain would promise not to sell her, then why wouldn't he let the other children go free once they reached Virginia? He had done a terrible thing by imprisoning them on this ship, and maybe his heart had softened since her mother's death. He had been nothing but kind to Kimberly since her mother had died.

"Will you let the others go free, too?" she asked, shyly meeting his gaze. "You were so gentle in your respect for my mother, I thought you surely must be a Christian man. And if y'are a Christian, you cannot be willing to profit from the misfortunes of others—"

A wall seemed to come up behind the captain's eyes. "I cannot do what you suggest," he said. "Another man waits for the money these children will bring."

"But—"

"You cannot say I have mistreated them."

"Nay, I cannot. But they are prisoners—"

"They are free to move about their hold. 'Twould be dangerous for them to roam above on deck. I am a good master, Miss Hollis, and I'll thank you not to spread rebellion among the other children."

"I won't," Kimberly promised, her heart sinking. She wouldn't dare inflate the hopes of the others if the captain would not release them.

"Indenture is not a bad life," the captain said, standing to his feet. "They will work until they are of age, and then they will be free to make their own lives in the richest land on earth. Many an Englishman would give his

127

fortune to have this opportunity, Miss Hollis. Don't be forgetting that."

"Aye, sir," she whispered.

* * *

The hold was quiet as she climbed down the stairs. When she turned to face her fellow travelers, she found that every eye was fastened upon her. "Y'are leaving, then?" Wingate asked, serving as spokesman for the group.

Kimberly blinked in surprise. "How did you know?" she asked.

Wingate jerked his head toward Brooke. "Miss Big Mouth has big ears, too. She hid on the staircase in the companionway while the captain talked to you. We all knew you might be leaving the ship, and—well, we'll miss you when you go."

Their concern seemed to dull the cutting edge of her sorrow. Her mother had felt that God had placed them aboard the *Seven Brothers* for a purpose, and apparently that purpose was just beginning. "I'm not leaving," she said, rubbing her hands over her arms. She swiveled her eyes toward Brooke. "I'll be with you all until we reach Virginia. I've decided to follow the will of my father and meet him in Jamestown."

128

Brooke clapped her hands in delight, and Wingate grinned. Several of the younger children cheered, and Kimberly thought that even Thatcher's hardened face wrinkled in a slight smile.

Abigail stood and gave Kimberly a gentle hug. Kimberly returned it and then made her way to her favorite spot by the window.

Ethan was sitting there, and his soft brown eyes studied her face as she sat down. "I was going to say a kaddish for your mother," he said, crossing his legs. "Will you help me?"

Though tears jeweled her lashes, Kimberly gave him

a bright smile. "Don't say a mourner's prayer for my mother," she said, looking out the window at the bright blue sky. "For her, and for this voyage, we'll say a prayer of thanksgiving."

Ethan nodded. "I think she'd be pleased."

"Yea," Kimberly answered, lifting her eyes to the wide horizon that stretched before them. "I know she would."

WEEK
TWO
❌

Thursday, May 20, 1627

14

As seagulls cartwheeled in the open space between the sky and sea, Kimberly leaned out of the ship's window and inhaled the warm, earthy scent in the breeze. It had been three days since Captain Blade had said they'd reach the Azores. He predicted they'd reach the islands within two days, but weak winds slowed the ship's progress by a full day. *Why, Mama,* Kimberly thought, *couldn't you have stayed a few days more? Mayhap we could have found a doctor—*

Dark thoughts hovered at the back of her mind, and Kimberly shook her head, determined not to dwell on things that couldn't be changed.

Kimberly turned her eyes away from the gray-green gloom of the ocean and sank to the hard wooden planks of the ship. She sighed, and next to her Ethan lifted his brown eyes and gave her an understanding glance. "I miss her, too," he said, propping his elbows on his bony knees.

"In just a few days she became a mother to all of us, Kimberly."

"I know." Kimberly turned away from Ethan. She didn't want to be rude, but it was hard to hear the others talk about her mother with love when Kimberly missed her so badly. Mistress Hollis had been in heaven for three days. In one way, Kimberly felt as if her mother had been gone for about ten minutes—she kept expecting to hear that gentle voice, feel a soft touch upon her shoulder, or see her mother's warm smile from across the ship's hold. But in another way, she felt as if her mother had been gone two years. She hadn't slept much since her mother's death and burial at sea, and at night, as Kimberly stared at the black sky and equally black sea, the hours crept by as slowly as an inchworm on a summer leaf.

"Kimberly," a familiar voice sounded. She turned toward the sound and saw Wingate Winslow, probably her best friend aboard the ship. He was frowning at a large pile of sailcloth in his lap. "Squeege said I should sew these two strips together," he said, nodding toward the canvas covering his legs. "And he gave me these things. But I have no idea how to use them."

Kimberly glanced over at the small box of tools next to Wingate's side. In the small wooden box were a bull's horn that had been filled with wax to hold thin sewing needles, several metal rings, a leather strap, and a long wooden stick with a pointed end. Kimberly leaned forward and fingered the tools, then shrugged. "I don't know a thing about sail making," she said, too wrapped up in her thoughts to really care about Wingate's problems. "Ask Abigail. She's the sempstress."

"You're right. Hey, Abigail!" Wingate yelled, and Kimberly deliberately blocked the sound of his voice from her ears. How could the others go on as if nothing had happened? She had lost her mother, the only parent she'd known for the last seven years!

Maybe the others didn't understand because most of them were orphans. Even Brooke, who had living parents, hadn't spent much time with her mama and papa because they traveled often and left her with a nanny. The others had their own heartrending stories. Disease, starvation, and unemployment had done more than destroy London's economy—it had also wrecked its families and sent thousands of men, women, and children out to live on the lonely, gray streets. A small voice of compassion quieted the anger in Kimberly's heart: Most of the others had lost their parents long ago. They understood hurt and loneliness.

When she learned that her mother was sick enough to die, she had tried bargaining to make things better. "Please, Mama, if we go back to London we'll get a doctor, and things will be fine," she'd said, but her mother only shook her head. Then Kimberly had denied how sick her mother was, certain she'd get better. But she didn't. She began to cough up blood, and that's when Kimberly realized the truth. And though sometimes she felt angry, she could not forget her mother's soft brown eyes and her plea that Kimberly keep her faith in God and her hope in America.

She knew she ought to swallow her grief and get on with the business of living. That is what her mother would have wanted her to do. *Think of me and remember what I have taught you,* she could almost hear her mother whisper. *Trust in God, Kimberly, and in the words of the Scriptures that are hidden in your heart. Teach them to the other children. And give your father my love when you see him again.*

So whenever funny-sad memories of her mother arose and made her blink back tears, Kimberly thought of the future. Of Virginia, with untamed wilderness, wild savages, and riches for anyone brave and strong enough to work hard. Of her father, the man she hadn't seen since

135

she was seven years old. And then she wondered what the years ahead might bring.

"Land ho!" one of the seamen called from the deck above, and the children lifted their heads toward the windows as if they were all pulled by an invisible string. In the distance Kimberly could see a cluster of islands rising from the flat ocean like brown, humpbacked turtles.

"The Azores," Ethan said, rising to his knees beside her. He and his family had traveled throughout the world to establish schools for Jewish students, and Kimberly had always been impressed with his knowledge. "The Azores are a group of islands belonging to Portugal."

"How many islands?" Kimberly asked, straining to see ahead.

"Nine, I believe," Ethan answered. "The largest is São Miguel. We will probably anchor there."

* * *

Thatcher thought that even the air seemed to be holding its breath as the ship approached the largest island. Five other ships stood at anchor in the harbor, and the waters were dotted with small boats rowing back and forth between the large oceangoing vessels. He felt a tingling sparkle begin at his toes and move up through his body as he studied the unfamiliar flags on the ships. How wonderful it would be to spend a lifetime on the oceans! To visit foreign ports and be free to go wherever the wind led!

Freedom was one reason he'd come aboard the *Seven Brothers*. He'd heard about the seamen who were picking up children from London streets, and Thatcher knew he was too quick and too smart to be captured or deceived by any of the sailors' tricks. So he'd followed a dark pair of sailors, hidden until he overheard the purpose of the voyage, and then he had walked aboard Captain Blade's ship as calmly as a choirboy. Any life, even an uncertain one in the wilderness of Virginia, was vastly preferable to the cold and squalor of London's streets. For six years Thatcher had lived by foraging half-rotted food from barrels of waste and snitching the fat purses of gentlemen. He was tired of stealing and running and hiding from the magistrates, tired of seeing pretty English women cross the street when they saw him coming.

He knew he didn't look like much. His clothes were a collection of old clothing from the trash pile, and the wooden soles of his shoes had long since worn away. His hair hung long and straggly down his back, and the features of his face were as sharp as his temper. The aristocrats of London had avoided him; the working people called him names and threw rotten fruit at him if he dared to linger near the doorsteps of their houses.

But on board the *Seven Brothers*, where he least expected it, he had been surprised by a spark of kindness. Mistress Mary Hollis had come aboard with her daughter, and though the lady was bewildered at the sight of so many children, her brown eyes had softened when she smiled at Thatcher. There was no disapproval or harshness in her glance or in her words. She was full of kindness and wisdom, and the illness that was consuming her strength and body could not touch the sweet spirit inside her.

137

He had tried to be nice to her. He had given her his scrap of blanket, his favorite place in the ship, and his time and attention. He heard every cough, every murmur, every sigh that passed her lips. And when she died, the secret hope that she had brought to life within him died, too.

Now he wanted only to leave this ship. He shouldn't have allowed himself to become all mushy and sentimental. He should never have concerned himself with Mistress Mary Hollis. Now she was dead, like everyone else he had ever loved. So he would never love anyone again.

"Thatcher."

A voice rang behind him, and for an instant he thought Mistress Hollis had returned from heaven, so much was the voice like hers. But then he remembered the daughter. It was she who spoke to him now.

He turned toward her slowly. "Aye? Why are you bothering me?"

Kimberly shrugged and waved her hands in a helpless gesture. "I'm sorry, I didn't mean to bother you. 'Tis just that I thought you might know something about what we'll do here and—" Her voice broke off, and she stared at the floor as a blush heightened the color in her cheeks. "In truth, Thatcher, I just wanted to talk to you. You've been so quiet these last few days."

"And I'd like to remain so," Thatcher said, turning from the window. He hated to leave the sight of the bustling harbor, but if he didn't, he'd have to stay and talk to Mistress Hollis's daughter. And right now he couldn't stand to look at the girl's face because Kimberly's coffee-colored eyes and golden brown hair reminded him too much of her mother.

Abruptly, he turned and walked away.

* * *

138   Kimberly sighed in exasperation as Thatcher left. What had she done to offend him? She scratched her head, thinking. She hadn't been exactly sweet and gracious to anyone since her mother had died, but she hadn't been mean to anyone either. She'd only wanted to sit alone and think. But the time for thinking was done. The other children looked to her for guidance now that her mother was gone, and she didn't know what to do with them. But Thatcher was as old as she, and he ought to be willing to help.

She lifted her chin in determination and followed him through the crowd of children. He had gone to the starboard side of the ship and stood before the other row of open windows. His eyes darkened when he looked down and saw her again standing beside him.

"What do you want now?" he snapped, looking away toward the water.

She took a deep breath. "My mother truly thought God put us on this ship for a reason," she began. "He could have put us on any ship in the country, but he chose this one. She thought 'twas because these children needed someone to help them on the journey."

"So?" Thatcher snarled, not looking at her.

"Well," Kimberly went on, praying that her voice would not break. "Now that my mother's gone to heaven, someone else will have to help these children. There are so many, Thatcher, and so many of them are young—"

"'Tis not my fault they are here."

"Nay, 'tis not." She paused, searching for words. "But mayhap God has put us aboard this ship to help the others. You and I are among the oldest, Thatcher, and you have lived on the streets. You know things that I do not, and the others look up to you. You showed real courage and compassion when you helped my mother—"

"I ain't no saint." He looked at her then, and his face was clouded in anger.

"Nay," she answered, cautiously feeling her way. "None of us is perfect. But you're clever and courageous, and you know your way around the ship."

"So what do you want me to do?" he said, folding his arms. "Lead all of ye in an escape? Toss the little ones overboard so ye won't have to worry about 'em?"

Kimberly felt her temper begin to bubble. This boy could drive anyone crazy, and yet she was trying to convince him to be a leader. "I think even Captain Blade likes you, though I have no idea why," she went on, her words biting into the silence between them. "You're rude, crude, and rough, and you have no respect for anyone who's trying to do what's right."

139

"And that's you, right?" Thatcher said, blazing down at her. "You're Saint Kimberly, and you're going to make all the others do whatever you say and wash their hands and eat their food and say their prayers like good little angels. And you think God will crown you with riches and glory for all you've done. Well, I've news for you, Saint Kimberly. God doesn't care what happens on this ship, haven't you noticed? We nearly perished in a storm. Your mother died without a doctor or anyone to help—"

Kimberly gasped, and Thatcher suddenly stopped, his face red and blotchy. Kimberly turned from the bitterness in his words and held on to a beam in the wall. He was cruel to remind her of her mother, and he was wrong to blame God for the storm and her mother's death. But what could she say? She had questioned God herself.

She left Thatcher standing by the window and went to find Wingate.

* * *

"Come to!" Thatcher heard the captain roar from the deck above. "Drop anchor!" The heavy cable that was wound around the capstan thrummed as it played out and allowed the anchor to splash into the sea and sink to the ocean floor. "Furl the sheets!" Thatcher closed his eyes and pictured the activity above on the deck. The sailors were climbing into the rigging, taking in the sails that had brought them to this place.

"Lower the shallop!" Captain Blade called, and Thatcher's eyes flew open. They would take the shallop, a smaller boat, to the island for supplies. If, perhaps, the captain could use an extra pair of hands, Thatcher could escape this ship. Even if it was just for an hour, it would be worth the risk of asking. He was not used to being cooped up like a bird in a cage.

Without another thought, Thatcher ran from the window and scrambled up the narrow staircase that led to the upper deck. A trapdoor barred his way, but Thatcher beat on it with the palm of his hand. "Captain Blade!" he called, a note of frustration in his voice. "Open up, I pray you!"

The door vibrated softly as a weight was dragged from atop it. In a moment the hatch lifted, and the bosun's heavy face appeared in the opening. "What's this bellowing?" Squeege asked, peering past Thatcher into the hold. "Is there trouble amongst the cargo?"

"No trouble," Thatcher answered. He climbed quickly up the remaining steps so Squeege couldn't drop the trapdoor, then looked the man straight in the eye. "Take me ashore with you, Master Squeege. I'll be a help, I promise. I know the captain could use an extra pair of hands to bring supplies aboard."

The bosun's wide face erupted into a grin. "So, 'tis Master Squeege now, is it?" he asked, laughter rippling through his voice. "When you want a favor, I'm of a sudden your master?"

"If you take me ashore, you will be," Thatcher answered, grinning back. "But if you don't take me ashore, I'll go bloomin' crazy down here in this hold." He lifted an eyebrow and gave Squeege a determined look. "There's no tellin' what I might do down here if I go mad."

141

Squeege looked away for a moment and thoughtfully scratched the stubble at his chin. "All right," he said finally, lifting the trapdoor higher. "But you'd better give me no trouble, or the captain'll flay both our hides."

Thatcher stifled his triumphant cry as he scrambled across the deck. The sails upon the three tall masts of the ship had been reefed, and the seamen were busy securing the layers of canvas. Just off the port bow, the shallop bobbed in the water. The captain and a half dozen of his men were already aboard.

"The boat's in the water already," Thatcher said,

pausing at the rail that ran around the upper deck. "How am I supposed to get down there?"

Squeege grinned so broadly that Thatcher could see the blackened teeth far back in his mouth. "Why, you jump in and swim, of course," the sailor answered, and Thatcher's heart turned to stone in his chest. Why, he'd sink like a rock! He couldn't swim. Never in his life had he been submerged in water. He'd never even had a proper bath.

But before he could protest, a strong hand grabbed the fabric of his shirt and lifted him above the railing. "Captain Blade!" Squeege called, hauling Thatcher over the rail. "One of the rats from below is thinkin' he'd like to go for a swim!"

"Nay!" Thatcher screamed, thrashing like a trapped cat in Squeege's grasp. But it was no use to protest, for in the next moment he was held aloft and dropped. The blue-green water rushed up to meet him, then covered his head in liquid shadows.

* * *

Kimberly and the others heard Thatcher's scream and the splash. As they hurried to the port windows, another splash slapped against the sea. Kimberly bit her lip as her eyes searched the waters. Two sets of steadily enlarging rings drifted over the surface near the captain's boat, then two heads rose through the water. Squeege appeared first, an impenitent grin on his face, and then he yanked Thatcher from below.

Kimberly relaxed when she heard Thatcher's frantic gasps. He was alive, thank God, and would remain so. She should have known Squeege wouldn't let him drown.

Squeege's loud laughter echoed over the quiet harbor, and the seamen aboard the boat laughed, too, as they hauled the two dripping latecomers aboard the shallop.

"Beshrew this, why'd you bring the boy?" Captain Blade asked, a trace of annoyance in his voice.

Squeege shook the water out of his hair and jerked his thumb toward Thatcher, who sat pale and still between two sailors. "I thought it'd be good to let him have a look around, that's all. I'm thinkin' mayhap this boy has the sea in his blood."

"'Tis more likely he has the sea in his lungs," Captain Blade answered, lifting an eyebrow. He leaned toward Thatcher. "Can you swim, boy?"

Kimberly could see Thatcher's proud frown even from the window of the ship. "I didn't drown, did I?" he answered, lifting his chin even though he shivered.

The captain's sour expression cracked into a smile. "Nay, you didn't," he said, then he barked an order to the seamen at the back of the boat. They began to row the shallop toward shore, and Kimberly and the others watched in silence as the captain and his crew made their way to the island.

"What will they do there?" Kimberly asked aloud.

Wingate, who stood by her side, followed her glance. "We need supplies," he said simply. "I heard the bilge boys say that much of our water spilled in the storm we passed through a few days ago. And we can't be forgetting that our Brooke tossed the captain's compass and maps into the sea, can we?"

143

From where she sat, Brooke overheard Wingate's comment and flushed in embarrassment.

"I said I was sorry," Brooke said, tossing her blonde curls. "And mayhap the captain's gone ashore for bread or fresh fruit. Has anyone considered *that* possibility?"

"'Twould be nice," Kimberly answered, wondering if they'd actually see any fresh food. If there were any, it was more likely the captain and his men would eat it. After all, she was still a child and the other children were only cargo.

Perhaps Thatcher would get a bite of fruit, since he was with the captain. Kimberly closed her eyes and imagined the sweet taste of an orange upon her tongue. If Thatcher was lucky enough to taste an orange, she was certain he wouldn't share it with the others.

Kimberly sighed in frustration. She had hoped he would become her friend and ally on the ship, but he showed more interest in joining the seamen than in helping her.

But Kimberly was certain God had placed her aboard the *Seven Brothers* for a reason. And just as her mother had planned to take care of the crowd of children aboard the vessel, Kimberly would do her best to act her mother's part. She'd tell stories as her mother had, and she'd teach the younger ones everything she knew about Virginia. With or without Thatcher's help, she'd do all she could to make this voyage more bearable for everyone.

15

Thatcher jumped out of the shallop and splashed through the shallows in open delight. It felt good to have land under his feet, and he stood uneasily for a moment upon the solid earth. Behind him, Squeege laughed. "The ground feels strange after you've gotten your sea legs," he said, slapping Thatcher on the back as he staggered through the sand toward the bustling settlement beyond. "Come on, me boy, you'll get the feel of it soon enough. Let's see what the Portuguese have here to make a man's day more pleasant."

A city rose into Thatcher's sight beyond the crest of the grayish brown beach, and as they neared it an assortment of sights and smells assaulted his senses. Gaily striped awnings covered an open-air market; baskets of lemons and oranges in one booth sent a zesty tang through the air. Sweet incense burned in brass bowls, and men crouched over low iron braziers where meat sizzled atop glowing coals. The smells of food and fires rose up to meet Thatcher, and after days of the close atmosphere of the hold, he breathed deeply and enjoyed the variety of scents in the wind.

Not only were the smells of this place different, but he had never seen such people. Dark-skinned and dark-haired, these merchants and men of the sea wore bright shirts of red and purple and pink, while golden belts held their swords and daggers ever ready at their sides. They moved with sudden, quick grace while they chattered endlessly in tongues he couldn't understand. Chickens clucked in woven baskets. A pair of goats bleated endlessly as merchants and seamen eyed each other and struck their bargains.

Captain Blade and his men moved through the market with ease, and Thatcher remained a few steps behind Squeege, more nervous than he wanted to admit. Squeege paused for a moment to talk to a pretty girl whose dark eyes smiled at him, and while they tried to understand each other, Thatcher glanced about. No one had paid him the slightest bit of attention, probably figuring that he was merely a harmless cabin boy. *What a life I could have here if I slipped away*, Thatcher thought, drinking in the delicious aroma of the fresh meat that sizzled on a nearby grill. *Bargaining with seamen in the daytime, snatching whatever I need to survive, hiding until the seamen leave port and then meeting a fresh shipload of sailors on the morrow. . . .*

The gleam of a gold earring caught Thatcher's eye. The man who wore it was tall, with sun-streaked hair pulled into a braid that fell down his broad back. He wore dark breeches and a full white shirt with billowing sleeves that ended in clean cuffs at his tanned wrists. A wide belt encircled his narrow waist, and from that belt dangled a bulging leather purse.

Thatcher's eyes narrowed as he studied the purse.

146

The man must be wealthy, for his clothes were fine, and
Thatcher could see the definite shape of gold coins
through the soft leather moneybag at the man's waist. He
held his breath and watched the man, who ran his hands
carelessly over the leather goods in a merchant's stall. He
had a certain smugness and self-confidence about him,
the air of the lazy and well-to-do, and Thatcher had often
encountered that attitude among the gentry on the streets
of London. Surely such a man deserved to lose his gold. If
he had not worked for it, why should he keep it?

A thin mongrel dog wandered up and sniffed curi-
ously at the stranger's boot. In a heartbeat, the heavy boot
shot out and kicked the dog away, and the dog's wounded
yelp cut to Thatcher's heart. *Why, this man is truly a scoundrel! Not only is he rich and lazy, but he has no more concern
for a homeless dog than for a bothersome mosquito!*

Thatcher gritted his teeth and clenched his hands.
He would take the man's moneybag and buy that poor
dog a decent slab of meat from one of the merchants.
Then he'd spend the rest of the money on whatever
caught his fancy, and if the rewards were good enough,
maybe he'd manage to get lost on this island and avoid
going back to the *Seven Brothers.*

He did not have a blade to cut the tie, so this would
not be a quick snatching. The man would know he'd been
robbed, but it would be easy to pull the moneybag and
run. With one quick jerk Thatcher could be away, and
probably this man could not run quickly, for his boots
were heavy. The element of surprise would work in
Thatcher's favor, and so would his quickness, for no one
in London had ever caught him.

He left Squeege talking to the pretty girl and crept
as silently as a shadow toward the man with the purse.
The marketplace crowd jostled him, but the stranger did
not move from where he studied a piece of fine leather in
the tanner's booth. If Thatcher were to act, he'd have to

147

do it before the man reached for his purse to buy the leather.

His hand closed around the soft calfskin of the purse without pulling upon it. He closed his eyes and took a deep breath to calm his pounding heart. He would yank it and fly away as he had done a thousand times in London.

But an iron grip closed around his wrist. Thatcher's eyes flew open and he jerked back, trying to flee, but the hand held him like a vise.

"What do you think you're doing?" a voice snarled. Thatcher blinked in surprise. The tall man with the braid had reached behind and caught Thatcher's hand without even turning around. *'Tis as if he has eyes in the back of his head!* Thatcher thought, confused.

The man turned slowly to see what he had caught, and Thatcher gulped. The man who held him had a sharp, pointed face that seemed to be made entirely of muscles. He wore a blond moustache and side whiskers, though his chin and cheeks were clean shaven. His dark, hawkish face seemed never to have known a smile, and the sharp scent of an exotic perfume rose from his skin. Thatcher swallowed carefully and fought his rising terror. What in heaven had he done now?

148 The man swiveled his grip around Thatcher's wrist but never released the pressure of his fingers. "What were you doing with my purse?" he asked, lifting a shaggy brow. The iron fingers tightened. "In my business, we cut off a boy's hand if he dares to touch another man's purse."

Thatcher's mouth went dry, and a tiny whine of mounting dread came from his lips. He could not speak. The man stared at Thatcher, his lips curving with cruel confidence, until the boy's heart raced and his fingers fluttered with fear.

"Welladay, what's this?" Thatcher nearly melted in relief when he heard Squeege's rough voice.

"I didn't do nothing," Thatcher said, finding his

voice. "Tell him, Master Squeege. He can search my pockets if he likes, but I didn't take nothing of his."

The stranger's grip did not relax. "You had your hand on me moneybag," he said, balefire in his dark eyes. "I felt it. You would have taken it and run."

"Why, you are of certain mistaken," Squeege said, easing his vast weight in between the stranger and Thatcher. "For where would the boy have run? He has no place to go but back to our ship. He has no place to spend whatever gold you may have in your purse."

The stranger's stern expression did not change, nor did his eyes leave Thatcher's. "I know a thief when I see one," he remarked in a cool voice. "And this boy's heart is as black as any knave's."

The words cut Thatcher like a slap, but Squeege gave the man a grudging smile. "Then let his knave's heart be on my head, and release him. You have your gold, and there's no harm done. I'll take the boy with me and promise you that this will not happen again."

The cruel grasp instantly loosened, and Thatcher's hand fell to his side. The skin where the stranger had held him was pinched and white, and Thatcher rubbed his sore wrist as Squeege continued to smile upon the stranger.

149

"What ship are you from?" the stranger asked, abruptly transferring his glance to Squeege's face.

"The *Seven Brothers*," Squeege answered, a touch of pride in his voice.

"An English ship?"

"Aye, thank God."

The briefest of smiles flitted across the tall man's dark face, and he snapped his fingers. "Of course! Your captain is Roger—"

"John," Squeege interrupted. "John Blade. Do ye know him?"

"Aye," the stranger said, smiling more broadly now.

"We met some months ago at a port on the Thames. Tell him I have said hello and that I will call upon him when I can." He turned as if to go, then doubled back. "How long will you be in this port?"

"We will make sail tomorrow, probably after noon-time," Squeege answered.

"Very well then," the man said, tipping his hat as he moved away. "Give my regards to your captain."

"But your name?" Squeege called, lifting his hand after the man.

Still moving away, the stranger turned around and smiled. "Tell your captain that he will hear from Delmar de Chavez."

* * *

Thatcher sat in the back of the shallop as the oarsmen rowed back to the ship. After saving his hide from the man in the marketplace, Squeege had not stopped scolding Thatcher. "I don't know how you lived in London," Squeege said over and over, "but you had best mind your manners on the sea, my boy. Many men will chop off your hand before asking if you mean to steal or to point the way."

150 Now Thatcher rolled his eyes as Squeege told the story to Captain Blade. "He told me he might come out to visit you, as he is a friend," Squeege explained. "Delmar de Chavez. He says he met you in London."

Captain Blade shook his head. "I know no one by that name," he said, leaning back against the side of the shallop to feel the sun on his face. "But it rings in my memory nonetheless. If he comes alongside, Squeege, welcome him, but don't let him aboard. We will see what sort of man he is."

"He's a sailor, no doubt," Squeege said. "He wears the earring, and his eyes are narrowed from scanning the sea. A tough man, he is, and our boy Thatcher here is lucky to have escaped with his hand still attached."

Thatcher rolled his eyes again and wished he could swim. He'd rather jump out of the boat and swim back to the ship than have to endure Squeege's unending lecture. But he wasn't a swimmer. Not yet, at least.

* * *

While ashore at São Miguel, Captain Blade had bartered for barrels of fresh water and two tubs of lemons and limes. Kimberly was surprised when the Captain and Squeege brought the tubs of fruit into the hold where the children lived. "Each of ye shall eat one fruit," the captain said, a dark warning in his voice. "No more and no less, till everyone has eaten."

"I don't like lemons and limes," Brooke protested from her corner. "They're sour. Could you not bring us a barrel of oranges?"

The captain scowled in Brooke's direction, and she promptly hushed. "If you want to live long enough to reach Virginia," Captain Blade went on, "you will obey me. Peel the fruit with your hands and eat every bit of the pulp." With that order, the captain turned on his heel and climbed to the upper deck. Squeege followed without a word.

151

"Why are we to eat these?" Kimberly wondered aloud, moving toward the two tubs. She looked at Thatcher, who'd just returned with the shallop, but he avoided her glance and slunk into his favorite corner. "What's so important about eating these that the captain will kill us if we don't?"

"He won't kill you," Ethan spoke up from the window. "Disease might, though. Fruit will help prevent scurvy, a disease that often strikes those who sail on the seas. Captain Blade is right. We have to eat these before they rot. There won't likely be any more fruit between here and Virginia."

"Scurvy?" Kimberly's heart began to beat faster. If scurvy was at all like the disease that had killed her mother, it would be truly terrible.

"'Tis a horrible illness," Ethan said. "Men grow weak; their gums and noses bleed. Eventually they die. My family and I were on a ship once where half the crew and passengers died from scurvy before we reached our port of destination."

Kimberly reached into the tub and picked up a lime. "Who needs help peeling theirs?" she asked.

* * *

"Ahoy! Captain Blade!"

Thatcher sat up abruptly and rubbed the sleep from his eyes. The soft sounds of children breathing filled the dark hold, but someone had called from the waters outside the ship. He crawled on his hands and knees to the window and peered out into the inky darkness. A torch burned brightly in a man's hand; a shallop rode the gentle waves. Thatcher felt sweat bead under his arms when he recognized the man in the torchlight: Delmar de Chavez. As he promised, he had come calling. Why? Was he truly a friend of Captain Blade's, or had he come to take his vengeance upon Thatcher for the incident in the marketplace?

"Who goes there?" someone called from the deck of the *Seven Brothers*.

Peering through the darkness, Thatcher saw de Chavez smile. "'Tis a friend calling upon John Blade. Wake him, will you, and toss us a rope? I've a fine bottle with me, and a desperate need to talk over old times."

Thatcher heard footsteps pound overhead as the lookout hurried to wake the captain. In a moment, another pair of footsteps joined the first, then Captain

Blade's strong voice called out over the waters. "De Chavez? I do not recall making your acquaintance, sir."

"Ah, my friend John Blade," de Chavez called, his white smile gleaming through the night. "I pray and beg that you will not be inhospitable. Welcome me aboard, and let us drink to our health and compare our fates since we last met."

"I am sorry, sir, but I do not recall our last meeting."

De Chavez smiled as if he were forgiving a forgetful child. "I feared you would not, for you were much drunk that night, John. But I forgive your lack of memory and offer you a chance to barter with me. What cargo are you carrying today? Supplies, perhaps, for another of your English colonies? You are headed west, so it cannot be gold or tobacco."

"I do not need to barter for any other goods," Captain Blade answered easily, his voice calm and casual in the night. "Nor am I disposed to entertain guests after dark has fallen. We are making sail tomorrow, my friend, so I must bid you farewell. Mayhap we shall meet again."

"You will not share my bottle with me?" de Chavez asked again, lifting a heavy jug into the air. "I do not think you should send me away. I would not send you away if our situations were reversed."

153

"Even so, I must bid you good-night," Captain Blade called, and Thatcher sighed in relief that the captain had not allowed the oak of a man on board.

From the boat, de Chavez shrugged. "Till we meet again, then," he called, his voice a ghostly echo above the steady slush and splash of the water. "Godspeed, John Blade."

"The same to you," the captain called.

The oarsmen of the boat began to pull away, and the footsteps retreated overhead. But Thatcher did not leave the window until he was certain that the torchlight had moved far, far away.

Friday, May 21

16

Kimberly felt a spot of warmth on her cheek and absently swatted at it in her sleep, dreaming that a rat had scampered up from one of the lower decks. The warmth did not leave, however, and she finally woke and squinted through one eye. It was only the sun on her face. Daylight had begun to brighten the hold, and already some of the younger children were awake and playing quietly among themselves.

She pressed her hands against the hard wooden planking of the floor and lifted herself up. Flat on her back next to Kimberly, Brooke snored in a gentle, regular rhythm. Long, red creases ran up and down Brooke's pretty face from where her skin had been pressed to the planking. Kimberly sighed. She couldn't make fun of Brooke because she probably didn't look any better.

Kimberly stood and stretched, easing the stiffness from her bones. The sun glinted off the waters on the starboard side of the ship, and Ethan sat at the window, already busy with his morning prayers. She tapped him gently on the shoulder as she passed by.

Each child aboard the *Seven Brothers* had developed a morning ritual, a routine to make life on board the ship bearable. Kimberly's routine was simple. First she got up and stretched, then she checked the weather by looking out the starboard and port windows. Then she sat down next to Ethan to say her morning prayers, and when those were done she visited the children's privy, a small, private toilet area behind the companionway, where straw had been strewn around a chamber pot. The smell of sweat and the reek of filth threatened to knock Kimberly over each time she approached. She found it hard to breathe at all while in the dark corner, but the need for such an area could not be avoided. The small ceramic pot that sat upon the straw had to be emptied regularly, and since no one volunteered to do it, Kimberly had undertaken the task herself.

She gulped in a deep breath of air, leaned forward and picked up the chamber pot, and rushed toward the nearest open window. After the chamber pot had been dumped into the sea, she returned it to its corner. No matter how hard she tried to keep the privy clean, the rancid and nauseating stench grew stronger each day. The humidity from the open sea only seemed to strengthen the terrible odors.

When her bit of housekeeping was done, Kimberly sat in the center of the hold with her back to the huge mainmast that pierced the holds of the ship like a giant toothpick. The younger children scampered to her side and seated themselves around her skirts. Her mother had loved to tell stories, and Kimberly decided that she would follow her mother's example and tell stories to help the children prepare for a new life in Virginia. She knew a few things about that savage colony from her father's letters and from books about the New World her mother had insisted she read.

But today she thought she would help the others learn to feel at ease on the ship. She was halfway through the story about Noah and the ark when she noticed that Thatcher had moved to the port windows. He seemed to stiffen as he looked out across the harbor, and a frown settled upon his handsome features. Kimberly paused. Had he seen something that upset him?

"Go on, Kimberly," Christian urged, tugging on the edge of her skirt. His sightless eyes couldn't see Thatcher at the window, but Brooke did. She shot Kimberly a questioning glance, and as Kimberly continued her story, Brooke rose to her knees and crawled across the floor toward Thatcher.

She'll tell me if something's wrong, Kimberly thought. She cleared her throat and continued with the tale. "So Noah and his sons obeyed God and built an ark large enough to hold two of every animal and seven of every clean animal."

One of the boys made a small sound of disgust. "I don't believe it," he said, waving Kimberly away. "How could two elephants fit on a boat? With two of every other animal?"

157

"Well, we don't know for certain that Noah took full-grown animals," Kimberly said, shrugging. "God could have sent him two *baby* elephants."

"How could Noah have room enough for all those animals and enough food to feed them for an entire year?" another boy spoke up.

Kimberly scratched her head, and Ethan supplied the answer. "Many animals hibernate," he pointed out. "God could have put the animals into a deep sleep. They didn't eat while they hibernated, so Noah didn't have to worry about feeding them."

"And let's not forget, the ark was a huge ship," Kimberly said. She waved her arms to indicate the sides of the *Seven Brothers*. "The ark was much larger than this."

"So how did animals from all over the world come to Noah?" one little girl asked. "Animals live in so many different places."

Kimberly shrugged. "God gathered the animals himself," she said. "And mayhap the nations of the world were not separated by water as they are today. But God is God, and with him all things are possible."

"Someone's coming!" Brooke interrupted from the window. Her face was flushed with excitement as she turned to Kimberly. "A shallop, loaded with men. And one of them is truly handsome!"

Kimberly left Ethan to answer the younger children's questions about Noah and hurried to the window. A shallop was indeed approaching, and a striking man stood in the front of the boat, a bottle in his hand. "Ahoy, *Seven Brothers!*" he called as the ship neared. "I would have a drink with your captain before ye sail today!"

Kimberly turned to Brooke and crinkled her nose. "Captain Blade isn't really going to drink with that man, is he?" she asked. "We're supposed to be getting ready to sail."

"Who cares?" Brooke said, shrugging. "He's the most handsome man I've ever seen, Kimberly, and if we're lucky he'll come aboard. Do you think the captain will let him come down here? I'd love to get a closer look at him."

"Nay, you wouldn't," Thatcher said, and both girls turned to stare at him in astonishment. He would not say anything else, but pressed his lips together in the stubborn expression Kimberly had come to know well.

The shallop rocked steadily on the waters, and from above their heads, Kimberly could hear the low voices of Squeege and Captain Blade. "Do you think we dare let him aboard now?" the captain asked. "What harm could he do? We're almost ready to make sail."

"If he is a friend of yours—," Squeege said.

"I don't know him, I tell you. Unless I met him while I was drunk."

"Mayhap you did. And it would not be good to offend him now, if you are friends. He doesn't look so threatening in the daylight, now, does he?"

Kimberly tilted her head to look at the stranger in the boat. He didn't look at all threatening. He wore a pleasant smile and a clean shirt, and his hair gleamed like silver in the morning sun as if he'd spent lots of time outdoors. With a healthy and tanned complexion and a sure, straight smile, he looked like any respectable sea captain eager to wish another a pleasant voyage.

"Bring him aboard," Captain Blade said suddenly, turning from the rail. "I'll have a drink with him in my cabin, then we'll be off."

* * *

Nervous flutterings pricked Kimberly's chest as four strange men from the shallop climbed up a rope ladder onto the ship, but after a while she ignored the steady clomp of heavy boots on the deck overhead and settled down to continue her stories with the younger children. "Tell us another," Denni cried, and Kimberly smiled at her in appreciation. The twins, Daryl and Denni, did not speak a word of English when Kimberly first met them aboard the ship, but with every passing day they picked up a few more English phrases. Kimberly hoped that her stories were helping them.

"All right," she said, glancing at Thatcher's stony face. An idea sprouted in her mind. *Mayhap a tale would help him, too.*

She crossed her legs under her long kirtle. "I'll tell you a story my mother used to tell me whenever I was tempted to do something wrong. Once, in the fair city of London—"

"London isn't a fair city," Thatcher interrupted from the window. His arms were folded across his chest, and he scowled at Kimberly. "'Tis gray and dirty and cold."

"Not always," Kimberly replied lightly. She smiled to reassure the others and took a breath to continue. "In London, as I said, a woman and her daughter worked in a pie shop. One morning the woman decided to sneak into the master's pantry and steal a few things for her own kitchen. 'I will just take a little,' she told her daughter. 'But after many days of taking a little, we shall have enough to bake a nice pie for us.' So she waited until the master had gone out, then she went into the pantry and bade her daughter follow. 'Daughter,' says she, 'you must stand guard and call out a warning if anyone sees me.'

"The woman slipped into the pantry to scoop out a cupful of flour, and the daughter cried out, 'Mother, someone sees you!'

"Well, the mother looked around and saw no one, so she took her cup of flour and moved to the barrel of sugar. After another moment the daughter cried out, 'Mother, someone sees you!'"

160 "Bloomin' foolish daughter," Thatcher interrupted, "always ruining things for the mother."

"She wasn't ruining things," Kimberly snapped, wishing he'd be quiet and listen. "She was helping." She cleared her throat and waited a minute to gather the children's attention again. "After a while the mother moved to the jar of lard, and her daughter cried out, 'Mother, someone sees you!' The mother stopped her stealing and looked around, but saw no one. 'Why in heaven's name do you keep saying someone sees me?' she asked, glaring down at her daughter. 'I don't see anyone here but you.'

"'Yea, mother,' the girl whispered. 'I see you, and so does someone who watches from above.'"

Kimberly pointed heavenward, and the children's faces brightened in understanding. But from his corner Thatcher glared, and Kimberly couldn't help but feel the heat from his eyes. *He's probably mad because he thinks I'm preaching at him*, she thought. *He knows I want him to be an example for the others, but he won't do anything to help.*

She decided to ignore him and smiled when Daryl called out, "Tell us another!"

* * *

Thatcher gritted his teeth as Kimberly finished her tale. It was as if she knew about his attempt to steal the stranger's purse, but how could she have learned about it? Squeege couldn't have told her, and none of the other kids knew the story. But Kimberly had to know, and that's why she chose to rattle off that terrible little story about how a bloke shouldn't steal because the Almighty was watching.

He shivered. If Squeege hadn't told Kimberly, then who? No one, unless God himself told Kimberly about Thatcher's mistake. He knew she prayed a lot, talking to God about one thing and another. Did God talk back? Had the Almighty told Kimberly to warn him?

No, that wasn't possible. It was more likely she told that story just to make him squirm. But she'd done a good job, for with Delmar de Chavez up on deck with the captain and a pint-sized preacher down below, Thatcher had squirmed plenty in the last hour.

161

But he wasn't going to squirm anymore. He stood to his feet and ran his hands through his hair, then shook out his arms and legs as if he were preparing for battle. After taking a deep breath, he stalked forward through the crowd of little ones at Kimberly's feet. When he stood right in front of her, he looked down and shook a finger in her face. "You," he said, his voice trembling, "stay away from me. Leave me alone. I want nothing to do with you or your God, do you hear? Just stay out of my life."

Her face went blank, then a tinge of sadness filled her eyes. Mistress Hollis's eyes!

He turned from the sight of those brown eyes and went to a dark, smelly corner near the toilet area. No one would bother him there.

* * *

Kimberly waited until Thatcher had gone, then her eyes caught Abigail's, and her brows lifted a question: *What's his problem?* Abigail shook her head as if to say she didn't understand Thatcher either.

Brooke quickly jumped into the unspoken conversation. "Who put the fly in his soup?" she quipped, tossing her curls over a shoulder as she slid nearer to Kimberly. "Didn't Thatcher sleep last night?"

"I don't know what's wrong with him," Kimberly answered, taking pains to keep her voice low so Thatcher wouldn't hear. "He's been this way for days now." She took a minute to chew on the edge of her thumbnail. "And you know, I thought he was really going to be nice. He did some very kind things for my mother."

"He's been this way ever since your mother died," Brooke said, snapping her fingers. "It begins to make sense. Do you think he is mourning for her?"

Kimberly frowned. "Why should he? She was *my* mother, and if anyone is upset, 'tis me. I miss her terribly, but I just do the things I know she'd want me to do."

"I think he really liked your mother, Kimberly," Brooke said, "and he doesn't know how to behave now that she's gone. He's not strong like you are."

Kimberly continued to chew on her thumbnail and looked at Abigail, but the other girl only shrugged. "I should talk to him," Kimberly finally said. "And if, perchance, he truly does miss my mama, then mayhap I can help him understand that she's gone to heaven. 'Tis not like we'll never see her again."

Abigail nodded in encouragement, and Brooke sighed. "I don't think talking will help Thatcher," she whispered, but Kimberly stood up and hurried toward the smelly corner where Thatcher sat against the wall.

"I don't know why you're so upset with me," she said, rushing through her thoughts so she wouldn't have to breathe the sour air. "I'm only trying to help these other kids and give them hope. That's what my mama would have wanted me to do because that's what she wanted to do. They need someone to look up to, Thatcher, and I'd like them to look up to you—"

"But I'm a beggarin' thief, right?" Thatcher interrupted, his dark eyes gleaming toward her. "So you'll tell them stories and remind them that I'm nothing but a snitch—"

"I don't know what you mean," Kimberly interrupted, shaking her head. This conversation was not going the way she had hoped it would. "I don't know what you were before you came aboard this ship, Thatcher, but you can begin a new life now and live differently in the colony."

"What if I don't want to go to the colony?" His eyes glittered with rebellion, and for the first time Kimberly was afraid of what she saw in them. "What if I jump ship now and join up with a group of pirates? There are surely such men around, Kimberly Hollis, for all that you're not likely to think they exist—"

He stopped abruptly when the creak of the trapdoor shattered the stillness. Every child's eye turned toward the companionway when heavy boots thumped on the steep stairs.

163

17

Thatcher felt the blood drain from his face as the heavy boots descended. He knew those boots—they belonged on the muscular legs of Delmar de Chavez. He had come at last to take his revenge upon the boy who had nearly stolen his purse of gold.

He shrank back against the wall and hoped that the straw's stink would keep the devil de Chavez away.

The man stood at the bottom of the staircase, and the children huddled together at the sight of the stranger in their midst. Behind him came Captain Blade, and Thatcher could tell that the captain had drunk too much of the ale de Chavez had brought aboard. Blade's eyes were red, and as he waved an unsteady hand at the children in the hold he slurred his words. "Here they are," Captain Blade said, smiling drunkenly at his companion. "Ready to be sold to the planters in Virginia. The man I spoke of stands to earn a great deal of money, and I have only to get them to Jamestown."

Delmar de Chavez did not seem at all drunk. He held himself upright, like a prince, and put his hands on his hips as he surveyed the children. Thatcher ducked low and tried to hide behind Kimberly. "No wonder you bought all that fruit to keep them healthy," de Chavez said, a smile in his voice. "Worth their weight in gold, are they?"

"Not in gold—in tobacco," Blade answered, grinning foolishly. "Though 'tis much the same thing. This one"—he pointed to pretty and plump Brooke Burdon— "this one has been an albatross about my neck, but she'll sell well in the colony." He giggled. "Sell well? 'Tis a rhyme."

"Aye, 'tis a rhyme," de Chavez agreed. His eyes swept the hold again, then Thatcher felt those dark orbs meet his own. The man's smile twitched. "I see you have recovered the use of your hand," de Chavez said, and Thatcher's skin crawled when he realized the man was speaking to him. "I hope I did not cause you any pain."

Kimberly whirled around, arching her brows in surprise, and Thatcher wanted to crawl under the rank hay and die there. He didn't want anyone to know what he had done, and yet this man had practically told the entire ship of his humiliation.

De Chavez smiled again, then turned toward the captain and extended an arm. "Shall I help you up the stairs, my friend?" he asked, his voice like silk in the quiet of the hold. "Can you manage them?"

"Of course I can," the captain blustered, stumbling toward the staircase. He climbed up, none too steadily, and before leaving the hold, de Chavez turned to look at Thatcher one last time. "Till we meet again," he said, his words full of dark promise. Then he climbed up the staircase and disappeared.

166

* * *

"Who was that?" Kimberly demanded, turning to Thatcher when the two men had left. "Though he is devilish handsome, he made my skin break out in gooseflesh."

"He's evil," Thatcher said simply, total conviction in his tone. "His name is Delmar de Chavez, and he's not a nice man."

"His name means 'of the sea,'" Ethan inserted, coming over. He held his nose. "Can't we go somewhere else to talk? Why, Thatcher, do you sit over here?"

"Because I don't want to be bothered," Thatcher growled, but Kimberly sighed in relief when he stood and followed her and Ethan to another corner of the ship.

"Now tell us," Kimberly said, sinking into a circle where Brooke, Christian, Abigail, and Wingate waited. "Tell us everything you know of him. He seemed to know you."

Under the scrutiny of their eyes, Thatcher reluctantly told the story of how he'd hoped to steal the man's purse and run away on the island. "Last night de Chavez came around in his shallop, and Captain Blade wouldn't let him aboard," he finished. "Most of you were asleep."

"But today the captain decided he could come aboard," Brooke pointed out. "Why did he allow him today and not allow him last night?"

"Darkness," Ethan suggested. "Last night Captain Blade couldn't tell if there were other men waiting in the dark to take over the ship. We're not in English waters here, so no one's going to come to our rescue if we're attacked by pirates, or the Spanish, or even the Portuguese. Captain Blade was prudent and wise—"

"What about today?" Kimberly interrupted. "I don't think getting drunk on a stranger's ale is very wise."

"He could see that there were no other boats waiting in the water," Wingate pointed out. "And if they really were old friends like de Chavez said they were . . ."

167

"He didn't want to offend him," Ethan finished. He uncrossed his legs and stood up. "No harm is done, so why don't we forget him? My guess is that our captain has retired to his bunk with a headache, and Squeege will have us under sail before long."

"There he goes now!" Wingate said, pointing out the window. The shallop that had brought de Chavez and his men was moving away from the *Seven Brothers* toward a long, sleek ship that rested at anchor farther out in the waters. "The *Falcon Lady*," Wingate said, reading the name on the ship's bow. "She flies no flag. I wonder what country claims her."

"'Tis of no import," Kimberly said, choosing her words carefully. Thatcher seemed honestly upset, and she hoped to put his mind at ease and teach him a lesson at the same time. "Our captain's had a foolish fling with an old friend, and there's nothing more to be made of this. And, Thatcher, we hope you will think twice before going ashore and risking your hand to steal a purse you can't possibly use."

She lifted a brow as she looked at him, but he had turned away and moved back to the dark, smelly corner from which he had come.

168

18

"Anchor aweigh!" Squeege called, his robust voice cutting through the sounds of activity on the deck above. The stout pole of the capstan creaked in protest as it began to turn. The cables around the capstan hummed as they pulled the anchor from the bed of the sea, and Kimberly felt the ship break free of its mooring.

"Make sail!" Squeege cried next, and Kimberly joined the others at the open windows as the sounds of creaking cables and flapping canvas filtered down from above. By watching the shadows on the water, she could see the majestic sails rising high upon all three masts, and soon they bellied taut in the wind as the vessel spread her wings and began to move away from the island of São Miguel.

The *Seven Brothers* picked up speed as her bow cut a path through the gray-green ocean. Kimberly stood at the window and closed her eyes, grateful for the fresh breath of wind on her face. The moving air tasted like salt and sunshine and was a welcome relief from the hot, sticky atmosphere that had filled the cabin for the last two days. Seagulls called down from the sky, and she opened her eyes again to watch them cartwheel through the blinding dazzle of the sun's path on the sea. With a quiet breath, Kimberly wished that her mother were there to enjoy the sight.

"Arrugh!" A sudden cry from above interrupted her musings, and Kimberly leaned out the window in time to see Captain Blade heave whatever he had drunk into the sea. "Great Neptune," he muttered, wiping his mouth on his sleeve as he regarded the water with bleary eyes. "I thought I had given you every offering my poor stomach could provide."

She grinned and pulled her head back into the ship. Mayhap the captain would learn not to drink so much, especially when he was planning to sail. A thought gave her pause: *How had Delmar de Chavez charmed Captain Blade so easily?* Last night the captain had been suspicious and uncertain of the man, but an hour ago he had drunk with de Chavez as if the man were a long-lost brother.

170 She shook off her doubts and moved to the center of the hold, where several of the younger children had gathered in a circle, waiting for her to tell them another story. "I've been thinking," she said, taking a seat in the circle. "'Tis a long voyage to Virginia, and we're all apt to go a wee bit mad if we do nothing but sit here and stare at each other all day. Mayhap we should all have a job."

"What are we supposed to do?" Wingate asked, running his hand through his curly hair. "The captain won't allow us up on deck, and that's where the work is done."

"We can do other things," Kimberly said, leaning back upon the bulk of the main mast. She gave Brooke a smile. "You speak French, don't you, Brooke?"

The girl shrugged. "*Oui*, a little. I've had a French tutor for years."

"Then you could help Denni and Daryl learn to speak English," Kimberly said, pointing to the two French children. "They'll need to be able to speak English once they reach Virginia."

Brooke's face brightened. "I could do that," she said, her eyebrows rising in pleasure. "It would be fun."

"What about the rest of us?" Wingate asked.

"Well," Kimberly said, hugging her knees, "everyone has talents. Christian has a beautiful voice. He can sing to us."

"Sing?" Christian lifted his head. "The sailors sing all the time. They don't need someone else to make noise—"

"But their songs are terrible," Brooke said, crinkling her nose. "You ought to offer to sing for them. They might work better to your songs than to those horrible sea chanties."

"That's a good idea," Kimberly said, glad that the others were enthusiastic about her plan. "And, Wingate, you were doing a good job on the sails the other day. If you could teach some of the others how to mend sails, that job would keep you busy."

"Abigail's best with a needle," Wingate pointed out.

"Ah, but we need Abigail to help with our clothes," Kimberly said. She pointed to one of the smaller children, a little girl whose dress was coming apart at the bodice seam. "Since these are the only clothes we have, we'll need them to stay in repair. Abigail can help with that kind of sewing." She glanced over at the pretty girl, who never said a word. "Would you like that, Abigail?"

Abigail blushed beneath her freckles, but she nodded enthusiastically.

"You know what would really be wonderful?"

Brooke asked. Her cheek rested in her palm, and a dreamy expression had filled her eyes.

"What?" the others asked together.

"An hour on the upper deck," she said, her voice wistful. "Just an hour. To get out of this smelly hold, to feel the breeze and look straight up at the sky."

"You can always look out the window," Wingate said, pointing toward the open ports in the sides of the ship.

"'Tisn't the same," Brooke went on. "What would it hurt the captain to let us up on deck even for a little while? We could promise to be good and not get in the way of the seamen."

"He thinks we're cargo," Ethan pointed out, "not passengers. You don't let cargo stand outside to enjoy the view."

"But he knows we're people," Kimberly said thoughtfully. "Mayhap we need to remind him."

"By mutiny?" Brooke suggested, a devilish gleam in her eye.

"Cargo can't mutiny," Ethan answered. "All Captain Blade would have to do is not give us dinner for one day, and we'd be sorry we ever spoke to him."

172   "We'll see what we can do," Kimberly said. "But there's another job to consider." She grinned at the group. "Who is going to volunteer to clean the privy and empty the chamber pot?"

"Not me," Ethan said, waving her eyes away when she looked at him. "Don't look at me. That's a terrible job. No one will want it."

"Someone's got to do it, "Kimberly said, raking her bangs out of her eyes. "And I don't plan to do it from here to Virginia by myself."

"Let's make it a punishment job," Wingate suggested. "Whoever is unkind or mean to anyone else will have the job."

"I like that," Kimberly said, grinning. "Whoever begins an argument or picks a fight must clean the privy the next morning."

"Says who?" a voice snarled, and a shadow fell over the group. Without looking, Kimberly knew that Thatcher had risen to stand behind her.

"We're trying to accomplish a few things here, if you don't mind," Kimberly said loftily, not glancing back. "A few rules for the good of everyone."

"Rules!" Thatcher snorted. "I hate rules, that's why I ran away from England. You can't have rules on the open sea!"

"Oh yes, I'm afraid we must have rules on the sea," Ethan said, his brown eyes serious. "Captain Blade has rules for his men, and they know his word is law. If he didn't have regulations, the ship would founder, and we'd all be in mortal danger."

"Well, I'd wager the captain's rules are a sight more sensible than the stupid rules you will come up with," Thatcher said, moving round the circle to glare at Kimberly. "What sort of rules do you have? Are we punished for not saying 'Pray excuse me' after every belch? Or if I but look at you in anger, will you force me to empty the cursed chamber pot?" He crossed his arms. "I'd like to see you try to make me do anything!"

173

"Of course we won't have stupid rules," Kimberly said, keeping her voice low so the younger children wouldn't think they were fighting. "We'll just have rules that maintain order and decency. After all, we can't all do as we please without thinking of the others—"

"I have an idea," Ethan said, daring to interrupt. He cleared his throat awkwardly as the group focused their attention on him. "The Word of God says that of all the laws in the world, two are the greatest."

"I won't hear no Jewish laws," Thatcher said, thrusting out his lower lip.

"They are not only Jewish laws," Ethan pointed out. "The entire civilized world has adopted them."

"What are they?" Kimberly asked, leaning forward.

Ethan's eyes widened as he recalled the holy words: "And thou shalt love the Lord thy God with all thine heart, and with all thy soul, and with all thy might. Thou shalt not avenge, nor bear any grudge against the children of thy people, but thou shalt love thy neighbor as thyself."

Kimberly clapped her hands. "Those are good laws," she said. "If we love God and love each other, we should have no trouble on this voyage. Those are all the rules we need."

"And if I don't like those rules?" Thatcher growled.

"Live by them anyway, and no one will bother you," Kimberly said. "For we will all love you, Thatcher, whether you want us to or not."

A wounded look suddenly filled Thatcher's dark eyes, and he turned from the circle of children and retreated to his corner. Wingate cast Kimberly a questioning glance, and she shrugged, unable to make sense of Thatcher's mood. He was a strange one, that boy, and just when she thought she understood him, he changed as suddenly as the wind over the waters.

The trapdoor overhead squeaked, and the children rose to their feet, knowing it was time for dinner.

* * *

Dinnertime was a highlight of the children's day at sea, for it was the only meal they were given and the only time they were allowed out of their hold. As Kimberly climbed down into the dark lower hold where the ship's three "bilge rats" lived, her heart stirred in pity for the thin, pale boys who spent all their time on the lower deck, where the provisions were stored. Every day they stood behind the serving table and tossed a hard "sea biscuit" and a slab of dried beef onto tin plates for the crew and the children. Three times a week, if all went well, the bilge boys heated a thin gruel of brown gravy and ladled it over the hard biscuit. The food was not good, but the children had long ago learned that everyone from the captain to the bilge boys ate it, and no one was allowed to complain.

Today, though, the bilge boys added a slice of lime to each plate, and Kimberly eagerly licked the juice from hers, remembering Ethan's horrible warning about scurvy. She noticed that the others ate their fruit, too, and she glanced around at the barrels to see how much fruit the captain had been able to pick up in the Azores. The fruit probably wouldn't last very long, and they'd be lucky if they made it to Virginia without getting at least a touch of scurvy or some other disease.

Captain Blade leaned against a wall, his face drawn and pale, his plate untouched. Kimberly guessed that his stomach was still feeling the effects of the ale Delmar de Chavez had brought aboard. She carefully avoided the captain and walked over to where Squeege had leaned against a barrel to eat.

"You'll be glad to know that we all have jobs now," she said, holding her plate steady as the ship rolled beneath her feet.

"Jobs?" Squeege said. His eyes twinkled with merriment, and Kimberly felt her cheeks burn. He was not taking her seriously.

"Yea," she said, lifting her chin. "You can't expect a hundred people to travel to Virginia without having something to do. So we're finding jobs for ourselves. Abigail is going to repair our clothing, and I'm going to tell stories to the younger children while Brooke teaches English—"

"That's fine, girl," Squeege said. He paused to take a huge bite from his biscuit. "Just keep 'em quiet and steady, and the captain will thank you. We don't want a hold of squallering young'uns."

"We want *real* work," Kimberly went on. "Wingate wants to mend sails, and Christian would like to sing to the seamen. We could all do with a bit of fresh air on the upper deck, and we're willing to work for it. So you'll have to make allowances, Squeege."

The bosun pinned her with a long, silent scrutiny. "And who are you to be telling me what I must do?" he finally asked, lifting a bushy brow. "You seem to forget your station, missy."

Kimberly looked him straight in the eye. "Mayhap you have forgotten," she said, lowering her voice, "that I am not one of your captives. My mother and I paid the captain good money for our passage, so you can't be treating me like one of the others. Paying passengers have rights, and I'm not asking for much, just for a chance to prove ourselves so we won't go mad with boredom while we're locked up in that stuffy hold."

A flicker of a smile rose at the edges of Squeege's mouth. "You have a point, so I'm beggin' your pardon, miss. What sort of allowances did you have in mind?"

"You'll have to let Christian come to the upper deck if he's to sing for your men," she explained. "And unless you want to bring torn sails below to Wingate, you'll have to let him come up. And there are others who can do many things, but they'll have to be allowed to come up on deck—"

"No children on deck. That's the captain's order," Squeege said, brushing crumbs from his beard. "But mayhap we can make an exception for the blind lad, if he's really a singer. My men might enjoy someone else's music for a change."

"Will you tell the captain what we're doing?" Kimberly asked, giving him what she hoped was a charming smile. "And ask him if he'd consider letting a few of us up on the deck—mayhap two at a time. We'd be healthier, Squeege, and much happier, and he wants healthy, happy children, doesn't he? No one is going to buy a sick servant once we reach Virginia."

Squeege grinned. "You're a clever girl. I'll tell him your plans and ask if the blind boy can come up."

"And others, too, if he needs us," Kimberly insisted. "We all need things to do. It wouldn't hurt the captain to let us come out for a few hours of fresh air and sun, would it?"

"Nay, I suppose it wouldn't," Squeege said. "But at the first sign of trouble, or if ye gets in the way, 'tis down into the hold for the lot of ye. The captain's word is law, whether you're a paying passenger or not."

"All right," Kimberly agreed.

19

The ship settled into a steady rocking rhythm as the afternoon sun sank into the western horizon before the bow of the ship. Many of the children lay down to sleep, but Kimberly fought the drowsiness that threatened to engulf her. It would be easy to sleep the voyage away, disengaging her heart and mind from the others, but she felt that God had a special reason for placing her on this ship. She'd never discover it if she slept through the weeks at sea.

She went to the center of the ship and sat down by the mainmast. Crossing her legs under her kirtle, she clapped her hands to break the hot stillness of the hold. "Gather round if you can stay awake," she called, her voice strong and bright. "Lesson number one: Today we learn about each other."

"I already know more than I want to about these people," Brooke grumbled from where she lay. But she sat up and moved closer, and Kimberly smiled. Brooke had truly been a spoiled brat when she first came aboard the ship, but now she grumbled mostly from habit, not meanness.

Ethan, Wingate, Christian, Abigail, Daryl, Denni, and a crowd of younger children circled around to the center of the ship and faced Kimberly. "Today we're going to talk about our favorite memories," Kimberly said. "Nothing sad or terrible today, all right? Only good memories. Who'll be the first to speak?"

She looked around at the sea of faces, but no one seemed inclined to begin. Abigail blushed when Kimberly caught her eye, and for a moment Kimberly wondered if she'd made a mistake. Abigail couldn't talk. Had Kimberly embarrassed her by asking for the impossible?

Christian was the first to break the heavy silence. "I was sitting on a street corner one day," he said, smiling. His hand fumbled for the small tin cup that was never far from his side, and he held it up. "'Twas my job, ye know, to hold my cup out like this and sing. Every morning Nettie, the woman who took care of me, led me down to the corner and bade me sing, and every night she picked me up, led me home, and put me to bed. This was all I knew of life, day after day." He shrugged. "Some days were hot, some cold, some pleasant, some not so pleasant. And people stopped to listen, and if they liked my song, they put a penny in my cup. Once a gentlemen tossed in a shilling, but then someone else came up and took the shilling away from me."

"Is that your favorite memory?" Brooke asked in a bored tone. "Getting a shilling for your singing?"

"Nay," Christian said, "my favorite memory comes from a cold day when I was sitting alone. The street was quiet, for most people were in their houses, safe and warm by the fire. I had only a thin cloak about my shoulders, and the wind was fierce with cold. My fingers were stiff and so numb I couldn't feel the cup in my hand."

His face softened, and his voice dropped down to a whisper. "And I remember thinking that life was miserable and that no one but Nettie truly cared a thing for me. I was almost angry, sitting there in my darkness and the cold, when suddenly I heard a soft sound, and then something warm and furry jumped into my lap and curled there."

"A cat," Kimberly guessed. "I had a cat in London. Her name was Gretchen."

"Shh, let him finish," Wingate said, elbowing Kimberly. She clamped her mouth shut and waited for Christian.

"Aye, 'twas a cat, but I had never owned one," Christian went on. "Nor had I ever touched one. But suddenly a bundle of silk and satin fur lay in my arms, and the sweetest rumbling sound I'd ever heard filled my ears. The cat licked my cold hands and warmed them, then she curled inside my cloak and gave me her warmth. All the while she talked to me in that low, sweet sound."

"She was purring," Brooke said. "All cats do that."

Christian shrugged. "A cat had never purred around me. At the end of the day, when the sun's rays had left the streets and Nettie came for me, the cat jumped out of my lap and never came to me again. But for that entire day I had a friend who remained by my side. And that is my favorite memory."

181

Kimberly sat quietly, thinking of all the small pleasures she had taken for granted.

"My favorite memory," Brooke said, sitting taller so everyone could see her, "is the day my father bought a new team of Arabian ponies. He had the grooms brush the horses and harness them to our carriage, and then we went for a ride through the city. Mama and I got all dressed up in our best clothes, but Mama had another headache, and there was no one but me and Papa to take the ride. So the driver took the reins, and we set out."

She sighed and pressed her hands to her rosy cheeks, caught up in the retelling of her story. "'Twas a lovely spring day, and we were such a sight! They were white ponies with long necks, bright brown eyes, and braided forelocks and tails. The carriage had been polished so that I could see my reflection in its sides, and my papa looked so handsome in his plumed hat and lace collar! He wore a shoulder cape in red wool, and slit sleeves on his doublet, with ribbon epaulets at the shoulder." Her hands flitted over her own body as she described the outfit. "I was wearing a dress with a high linen collar with lace edging, and long gloves of fine leather. Mama had dressed my hair with ribbons and curls down my neck—"

"Is there a point to this story?" Wingate interrupted. "I don't care to hear about the fashion parade."

Brooke pursed her lips in a pretty pout. "I'm just setting the scene, mind you. That wasn't my favorite part. The favorite part was that my papa and I talked." Her cheeks flushed, and she pressed her hands together as she went on. "He asked me how I was doing in my lessons, and I told him fine, then he told me about Lord and Lady Ashland, whom he and Mama had just visited. And then he asked me about my pony, so I told him, and he said he'd always wanted a pony like that when he was a boy. . . ."

Brooke's voice faded away as tears trembled on her lashes. "'Twas one of the few days I can remember my papa talking only to me," she whispered. "'Tis my favorite memory and one I shall take with me wherever I go."

Kimberly felt a lump rise in her throat as she looked at Brooke. Though she could barely remember her father, she couldn't imagine life without ever talking to her mother. Her mother had always been by her side to teach her about life: how to be respectful to her elders, to pray and honor God, to look for the lovely things in the world. But even though Brooke had lived in a big, fancy

182

house with everything her heart desired, she had rarely spent time with her parents.

"I have a story," Wingate said, lifting his head. He waited until the others turned toward him, then he lowered his head to his knees and focused on a memory long past. "My mother was a housemaid for a fine gentleman and his lady in London. I grew up there, and I suppose I was sort of a pet for the other servants. But I always knew my place. We worked at the house, and though we lived in a small room at the back, we weren't part of the family. And when my mother died and I had to leave, I realized that I hadn't really been part of anything."

His voice thickened for a moment, but he cleared his throat and went on. "But my favorite, best memory was of a day when I was about six years old, I suspect. The master kept a barn at the back of the estate, and the stableman kept a cow for the master's milk and a sheep for wool. One morning in springtime, the stableman called me out to the barn and placed a lamb into my arms."

Wingate's face cracked into a twisted smile. "'Twas a little, squirmy thing, and 'twas so loud! It was crying for its mother, but the stableman said the ewe had died in the night while giving birth to the little one. He was about to kill the baby, too, because he didn't have time to feed a wee lamb, but he thought of me and said I might take care of it."

183

"You mothered a smelly, disgusting *sheep?*" Brooke asked.

Wingate lifted his chin in defiance. "'Twas a lamb, and clean and sweet," he said. "The stableman taught me how to help it drink from a skin filled with cow's milk, and I slept in the stable with it every night to keep it warm."

"You slept in the barn?" Brooke interrupted again, crinkling her nose in disgust. "In the hay?"

"'Twas cleaner and more comfortable than sleeping

on this ship," Wingate pointed out, pinning Brooke with a piercing glance. He had a point, Kimberly thought. Brooke shut her mouth and did not answer.

"In time, the lamb came to follow me everywhere," Wingate said. "When I went for a walk around the grounds with my mother, the lamb came along, too. When I helped the stableman clean out the barn, the lamb followed me. He had a funny, stiff-legged walk, and he'd frolic along behind me whenever he heard my voice."

Wingate fell silent, smiling, and after a moment Kimberly spoke up. "So that's your favorite memory? The lamb?"

"Yea," Wingate said, looking awkwardly down at the floor. "My frolicking lamb."

"What happened to it?" Christian asked.

Wingate's smile suddenly flattened out. "I don't know. One day I came home, and the lamb was gone. The stableman told me that the master had ordered him to sell everything but the cow."

Wingate and the others sat for a moment in the heavy hush, and Kimberly knew she ought to say something. She had wanted this time to be happy, not depressing.

"Denni?" she asked, looking toward the twins. 184 "Daryl? Do you have a favorite memory?"

The twins looked at each other, then turned to Brooke, who repeated Kimberly's question in French. "*Oui*," Denni said, her blue eyes lighting with excitement. A torrent of fluid words poured from her, and after a moment Brooke held up her hands.

"Slowly," Brooke said, laughing. "My French isn't *that* good!"

Brooke listened as Denni told a story, and Daryl interrupted occasionally until the tale was done. Then Brooke turned toward the others. "Their story," she said, tilting her head toward the brother and sister pair, "is about the day when their baby sister was born. They had been told that their mother was very sick. When she went into her room and began to cry, the twins thought their mother was of certain going to die."

Daryl interrupted Brooke for a moment, and Brooke listened, then murmured back to him in French. "He's afraid you won't understand that he was much younger," she said. "He knows now that babies are born through a woman's pain. On that day he thought his mother was dying. But after a while, his nurse brought Denni and Daryl into their mama's room. She was propped up in bed with a new baby in her arms."

"Carlotta Angélique Fortier," Denni told the others, her blue eyes beaming with happiness. *"Ma bébé soeur."*

"Carlotta Angélique Fortier," Brooke repeated. "Her baby sister."

"I did not have a baby sister," Ethan said, his voice a quiet murmur in the hold. "But I have a favorite memory I'd like to share."

The others turned to the quiet boy, and Kimberly knew they were more than a little curious about Ethan's life. Everyone knew he was Jewish, but few of them really knew what being Jewish meant.

"All of my favorite memories center around the Sabbath," he said, looking at his hands. "In the twelfth century a great Hebrew poet wrote that the Sabbath is the choicest fruit and flower of the week, the queen whose coming changes the humblest home into a palace. No matter where my family and I lived, when we celebrated the Sabbath together, I always felt like a prince in the home of a king."

"What is the Sabbath?" Brooke asked, her eyes wide.

"The seventh day," Kimberly explained. "One of the Ten Commandments tells us to honor the Sabbath and keep it holy."

"How do you celebrate the Sabbath?" Wingate asked. "To me 'twas a day like any other."

185

"Not in a Jewish family," Ethan said, shaking his head. "On Friday afternoon my father hurried home from work because the Sabbath begins at sundown. My mother spent Friday afternoon in her garden, gathering flowers for the Sabbath eve table. Just before the sun set, my mother would light the Sabbath candles and thank God for the commandment to burn the special lights. My brothers and sisters and my father would watch Mama light the candles. When the candles were lit, my mother would cover her eyes for a moment of prayer and whisper the ancient blessing. Then she would look at my father and say, '*Shabbat Shalom.*'"

"What does that mean?" Wingate asked, leaning forward in eager interest.

"Sabbath peace," Ethan answered. He sat quietly for a moment, lost in thought, then went on. "After my mother had lit the candles, my father and I would go to the synagogue service. At the service, we sang with great joy and peace in our hearts. We did not think about school, or the troubles of the world, or the bad things in our lives. We thought only of peace and rest. After the service we greeted the others with best wishes for a good Sabbath and hurried home. My father pronounced a special blessing over us as we sat at the Sabbath table and ate loaves of challah. He would wash his hands and recite the kiddush for my mother—"

186

"The kiddush?" Kimberly interrupted. "The prayer of mourning?"

"No, that's the *kaddish*," Ethan explained. "The *kiddush* is a prayer of blessing for the wife."

"That's nice," Brooke said. "I like that. Women deserve special prayers."

"After the kiddush, Father said the traditional blessing for the bread," Ethan went on. "After passing a piece to everyone at the table, we ate. Mama always made chicken soup, salad, chicken, and cake for dessert. After we ate, we sang special table songs known as z'mirot. They are songs of praise to God. After the songs, my family recited the bentshen, an after-meal prayer."

Ethan's brown eyes shone with sensitivity. "On Sabbath eve my family used our best dishes and wore our best clothes. 'Twas a time of celebration, a time when we put everything else aside and rested in God. No matter how poor our home, we always felt that we were royalty when Queen Sabbath was among us."

"Queen Sabbath," Kimberly whispered, imagining a cozy home where a mother lit candles and covered her eyes to pray for her loved ones. She could almost taste the soft, sweet bread and smell the chicken soup.

"My favorite memory is a little like Ethan's," she said, smiling at the others through a veil of tears. "Every night before bed, after a long day of work at the pie shop, my mother would loosen her hair, brush it, and pile it into her nightcap. Then she'd pull her Bible over to the stove and read to me by the light of the fire." Kimberly relaxed and leaned back upon the mainmast behind her. "She read the parables of Jesus and the Psalms. The Proverbs, though, were her favorite."

"Which ones?" Brooke asked, then she blushed. "My mother never read anything to me."

187

Kimberly smiled. "She liked the proverb that said 'tis better to eat a dry morsel in quiet than to be in a rich house full of strife. Our house was very quiet, and until she found work at the pie shop, there wasn't much to eat." Kimberly shrugged away the troubling memory. She was supposed to be thinking about the *good* things. "Mama also liked to say that a soft answer turns away wrath, but grievous words stir up anger. She quoted that verse whenever I lost my temper."

"I can't imagine you losing your temper very often," Christian said, smiling in Kimberly's direction. "You seem so calm."

"Not always, as some of you have already seen," Kimberly answered, looking at Brooke. Outside, the slowly paling sky threw long shadows upon the water behind the ship, and she suddenly felt very tired. Reliving old memories had its drawbacks, she realized. Sometimes it hurt to think of good times because once they were gone, they could never be recaptured.

Abruptly, she stood from her place and stretched. "I think I'm ready to sleep," she said, moving toward the open space near the window. "'Twill be dark soon."

"Pleasant dreams," Brooke quipped, rising to find her own place.

The group of children gradually dispersed, and as she settled down to sleep, Kimberly threw a quick glance toward Thatcher's dismal corner. Why hadn't he joined them in the circle of conversation? He was still in his place, unmoving, his dark eyes giving nothing away.

* * *

Thatcher waited until the others had quieted and stilled, then he rose and moved slowly through the hold, giving his much-cramped legs a stretch. He had thought about a thousand things that afternoon, determined to block the others' sappy and sweet stories from his mind, but still Kimberly Hollis's question haunted him: *What is your favorite memory?* He would never, ever share his remembrance with the others.

Still, the memory came crowding back, like an unwelcome and bothersome guest. His favorite memory was still shiny and new, for the event had happened right here on this ship. The most wonderful of all his hours had passed but a few nights before, not long after the ship had sailed from London.

One evening the ship had been quiet and dark, much like it was now, and he had been nervous about the journey and unable to sleep. He stood in the darkness and padded his way quietly through the hold toward the window, desperately seeking a breath of fresh air. He stood at the window for a long time, probably too long, and for a few moments he even considered jumping through the opening and into the waters below. Who would miss him? No one. Not a single soul would care that he had jumped into the sea. No one aboard the ship or in the streets of London would notice his absence. He was nobody, nothing, a nonexistent person who owned nothing and cared for no one. What had the rich man called him as he kicked Thatcher off the sidewalk and out of his way? *A worthless sack of skin.*

And then, just as his fingers had tightened around the rough wood of the windowsill, a quiet hand rose from the darkness and plucked at his sleeve. He paused, startled, and looked down to see Mistress Hollis sitting up in the darkness beside him. Her face was strained with fatigue, but seemed lighted from within as if something holy burned inside her.

She slipped her arm from his sleeve and patted his hand. "What a special lad you are, Thatcher Butler," she whispered, a shy smile curving upon her lips.

He gaped in amazement that the lady even remembered his name. He didn't answer her, but slipped back to his spot and sank into thoughtful reflection. Someone did know who he was, and if he jumped into the sea, someone would miss him. Mistress Hollis, sick though she was, had smiled at him with love and concern in her eyes.

In that moment Thatcher had known he could not disappoint Mistress Hollis. She thought he was special, and since she was good, she must think him good, too. Despite his past as a common thief, she saw him as something else, someone who could be unique and wonderful. He decided to believe her. He *was* special.

That memory was too precious and private to be shared with the others aboard this ship. It was more valu-

189

able than a story about a pony ride or chicken soup on Saturday, and Thatcher wasn't about to share it with anyone.

The memory was all he had left. Since Mistress Hollis was gone, Thatcher didn't feel so special anymore.

Saturday, May 22

20

The morning air was warm and burnished with sunlight when Kimberly opened her eyes and yawned. The ship rocked beneath her in a steady rhythm and nearly lulled her back to sleep. She turned onto her side, pillowing her cheek with her hand, but a sudden sharp scent crinkled her nose. "Ugh!" she muttered, opening her eyes. "What's that terrible smell?"

She lifted herself up on one elbow and blinked to clear the fog of sleep from her eyes. Across the hold, one of the boys was retching, his hand to his stomach. *Oh no,* she thought, lying back down on the floor. *Who'll want the job of cleaning up after him?*

"Kimberly!" Brooke's sharp voice cut through the quiet of the hold. Kimberly lifted her head and squinted toward the source of the sound. "Over here!" Brooke called, her blonde hair gleaming in the morning light. "They're all sick!"

Kimberly groaned as she pushed herself up off the floor. The children around Brooke were lying still and pale on the floor while a foul-smelling puddle pooled in their midst. "I can't stand it!" Brooke whined as she held her nose. "I'm afraid I'm going to—"

Her dainty face suddenly twisted into a grotesque grimace. "My stomach," she muttered through clenched teeth. "It—oh—"

"Don't," Kimberly pleaded. "Don't do it, Brooke. Just think happy thoughts."

"I can't," Brooke complained, clutching her stomach. "It hurts—oh!"

Kimberly whirled around and buried her face in her hands as Brooke followed the example of the other sick children. What was this? Had they eaten something bad? Would everyone be sick today?

Kimberly moved quickly toward the companionway, then she climbed the stairs and rapped on the hatch with her palm. "Help!" she called, hoping her voice would carry through the wooden planks. "Captain Blade! Mister Squeege! Someone's got to help us!"

The door opened slightly, and Squeege's broad face peered through the opening. "What's wrong with you, missy?" he said, frowning. "The captain won't like all this caterwauling."

"There's sickness below," she said, pointing down into the hold. "So many are sick, Squeege. Is there something you can do to help them?"

Squeege looked away for a moment, then lowered his eyes to hers. "There's nothing for me to do, missy. Men get sick at sea, too, and there's nothing to be done but wait. Whether it's yellow jack or bloody flux, we can only wait until the sickness passes."

Kimberly stared at him in astonished surprise. He wasn't going to help? Who was going to take care of all these sick children?

Something in her expression must have moved Squeege, for he reluctantly nodded and held his finger aloft. "Wait a minute, and I'll toss down a couple o' buckets for ye to clean up. Just wash down the decks when ye have to."

A moment later, Squeege handed Kimberly two rusty buckets with ropes around their handles. The buckets clanged together as they fell through the opening, and the rough rope burned her hands. Kimberly woodenly climbed back down into the hold as the trapdoor closed overhead.

She let the buckets fall onto the floor as she stared at the scene before her. Just yesterday this hold had been filled with a hundred healthy, talkative children, and today most of them lay flat on their backs or doubled over in pain with their hands clasped around their bellies. The stench of sickness threatened to choke the very breath from Kimberly's lungs, and her legs turned to jelly at the thought of walking through the crowd.

Her stomach tightened, but she didn't think she was sick. Her forehead was cool, her hands steady. *What would Mama do?* she wondered. Her mother would care for the sick and calm those who were frightened by the sight of so much illness. She'd clean up their messes and try to keep the sick ones comfortable. She wouldn't panic, and she wouldn't sit in a corner and do nothing.

193

If Squeege and the captain weren't going to help, Kimberly would have to take care of things herself. "Very well, God," Kimberly whispered, breathing a quiet prayer. "If you want me to do what my mother would have done, you'll have to give me strength and a strong stomach."

She took a deep breath and lifted her kirtle with one hand while she dragged the buckets behind her with the other.

* * *

From his corner near the privy, Thatcher woke to the sounds of retching and moaning. Sickness! So far they'd been lucky that they hadn't had much seasickness, but this morning it seemed as though everyone on the entire ship was determined to heave his guts into the open.

He sat up and felt his own stomach churn. He wouldn't be sick! He couldn't show weakness in front of the others. He'd just think of something else. He wouldn't think about food or the waves or the rocking, rolling movement of the ship. . . .

Kimberly Hollis was making her way through the crowd, trying to move the sick ones closer to the windows for fresh air. 'Twas just like a bossy busybody to disturb those who least wanted disturbing. But she wasn't being bossy, he had to admit. Her voice was gentle, and her hands were strong as she carried the young ones and helped the older ones to the window. Maybe she thought she could win the captain's favor by helping out. Or perhaps she was just pretending to care, making believe she was a great lady like her mother.

21

Kimberly helped the sickest ones to the window, then walked to the center of the hold to make an announcement. "Those of ye who feel a bit sick at your stomach," she called, waking those who still slept, "stay by the windows and rest there. If you are going to be sick, please lean out over the water. If you are not sick, come hither into the center of the hold and leave the windows to the sick ones."

A few pale-faced children slowly crawled toward the open windows at the sides of the ship, and others scrambled to the center, where Kimberly stood. Everyone seemed to find a place, she noted, but Thatcher. He remained in his favorite spot, the nasty-smelling corner near the privy. She knew him well enough to know that he wouldn't move anywhere just because she'd asked him to.

"All right then," she said, glancing down at the still-healthy ones at her feet. Among them were Denni, Ethan, and Christian. Denni kept tossing loving, concerned glances toward Daryl, who had stretched out by a window, and Kimberly didn't have the heart to separate them. "Denni," she said, tapping the girl lightly on the shoulder and then pointing to the other twin. "Why don't you stay with your brother?"

Denni's face brightened in gratitude and under-standing, and she scooted off toward Daryl. The others looked up to Kimberly for direction. "'Tis up to us," she said, rolling up her sleeves, "to keep this place clean and help the sick. My mama always said that sickness and dirt go together, so the floors must be kept clean no matter how many of us are ill." She pointed toward the buckets. "Ethan, if you and Christian can haul up fresh water, we'll dump it over the floors."

"The sick ones will get wet," Ethan pointed out. "Won't the water just run onto them?"

"Probably," Kimberly admitted, frowning. "But we have to sleep on these floors tonight, and I'd rather sleep on a wet floor than a filthy one."

Ethan nodded in agreement, and he and Christian took the buckets and moved through the sick children toward the windows to fetch seawater aboard. Kimberly looked toward the dark straw-filled privy. She didn't know why, but she had a clear feeling that the dirty straw should be removed and the chamber pot flushed out again. Her mother had told her stories from the Bible about how God had commanded the Israelites to keep themselves clean. The people of Israel attended to their toilet needs far outside their camp, and they were com-manded to wash their hands after handling anything unclean.

Why, then, couldn't the captives keep clean aboard ship?

Gulping in a deep breath of fresh air, Kimberly straightened her shoulders and hurried toward the smelly

corner, determined to gather up and dump the soiled
straw before her courage failed.

* * *

Thatcher lay his head back upon the hard planking and
groaned. His skin was clammy with cold sweat, his head
pounded, and his stomach writhed in his belly. Tiny
shooting pains flashed through his arms and legs, and no
matter how he twisted or turned, his body refused to be
comfortable. The floor beneath his skin was both coolly
inviting and repulsively slimy.

He didn't want to admit it, but he was sick, as sick as
the little ones who cheerlessly threw up whatever was in
their stomachs and lay down to rest before doing it again.
But if he went over to the window, Kimberly Hollis
would know he was sick, and she'd come over to check on
him like a fussing mother hen. He didn't want anyone to
fuss over him, especially her!

His stomach knotted and cramped suddenly, and
Thatcher groaned. He had no choice now. He had to go
to the window, or else dirty his favorite spot. He turned
over, gathering his strength, and stood up. The cabin
seemed to sway around him. Or did the floor suddenly
lurch sideways? He put out his hand to brace himself
against the wall, but the wall wasn't there, and he felt himself falling into empty space.

197

"Help," he managed to croak. Then he felt the floor
slap hard against his chin, and blackness surrounded him.

* * *

"You're sick, Thatcher. Why didn't you say so?"

He knew who spoke even before he opened his eyes.
It was Kimberly's voice, and he was sure that she sat next
to him with one of those rusty buckets at her side. He was
not going to lose his biscuits in front of her. He would
not be sick!

"I'm fine," he said, keeping his eyes shut. The ship couldn't swirl around him if his eyes were closed.

"You're not fine," she insisted. She must have pressed a wet cloth to his head, for he realized he felt cooler, and his head throbbed less. "You took a spill and knocked yourself out right in front of the others. What'd you think, that you could kill yourself and no one would notice?" The cloth lifted from his forehead, and he heard the sound of someone wringing fabric in a bucket. "So, what are you needing?" she asked, her voice softer now. "A sip of water? The bilge boys brought us up a bucket of fresh water, if you're wanting a drink. Or if you need help toward the window, Ethan and I can carry you—"

"I don't need anything," he snapped, daring to open his eyes so he could glare at her. She seemed to shrink back before the intensity of his gaze, but then the corner of her mouth dipped in a half smile.

"So say you," she said. "And I don't need anything either. None of us do. We're doing just fine out here in the middle of the ocean with no doctor and no clean clothes and no beds and only a wee bit of fresh water."

A spasm gripped his stomach, and he gritted his teeth, still determined not to show her how sick he was.

198

"Very well," she said, standing up. From where he lay on the floor, Kimberly suddenly seemed ten feet tall. She lifted the bucket of cooling water. "Since you don't need anything, I won't bother you. But if you need help, you know who to call."

"I don't need help," he snapped, closing his eyes again. When he was sure she had gone, he clutched his stomach and curled into a ball.

* * *

From across the hold, Kimberly watched Thatcher crumple beneath the pain. He'd probably feel better if he would just admit he was sick and allow the poisons to

leave his body, for the little ones who had been sick at
sunup were already beginning to regain their color and
energy. But Thatcher was too stubborn to admit he
needed help, just like he'd been too stubborn to help her
lead the others who were like the motherless lamb of
Wingate's story.

And she needed help, for she was tired. Her arms
and shoulders ached from carrying uncounted buckets of
water, and even though she'd washed her hands in the seawater at least twenty times, on her palms she still could
smell the rancid scent of the soiled straw from the privy.
Her kirtle was dirty and stained, the hem wet and bedrag-
gled from the continual sloshing Ethan and Christian
were giving the floors. Everyone was wet from the flood
of water, but the sick ones had fever and didn't seem to
mind, and at least the floors were clean.

She leaned against the mizzenmast for a moment,
too tired to care about anything. Squeege and the other
crew members had come down at dinnertime, but none of
the children had any appetite. The sick ones couldn't
keep anything down, and the healthy ones were too tired
from working and too nauseated from the odors in the
hold to even consider eating. Squeege had told Kimberly
that Captain Blade and a couple of the crew members
were sick, too. 199

"Will you tell us a story, Kimberly?" one little girl
called, and Kimberly felt her heart break at the pitifully
weak voice.

"A story?" she echoed, wondering if she had the
strength.

"Yea," another of the boys answered, turning onto
his stomach. He propped his chin on his hands and
waited for her to begin.

Kimberly sighed and raked her hair away from her
face. Wasn't it enough that she had to clean and carry
them? They wanted entertainment, too! She was about to

answer that she was too tired to tell a story, but then realized her mother would never have been too tired. Even
when she was very sick, Mistress Hollis had always found
time to tell stories to anyone who wanted to listen.

"All right," Kimberly said, searching her memory
for a quick, easy tale. "There's a story by Aesop about a
mouse and a lion."

She fully expected to hear someone cry out that the
story was old and familiar, but no one did. "One day a
lion caught a mouse in his paw and prepared to eat him,"
Kimberly said, propping her chin on her hand as she
looked around at her audience. "But the mouse said, 'Oh,
please, Your Majesty, don't eat me! If you will let me go, I
promise to help you someday.'"

The little girl laughed at Kimberly's squeaky imita-
tion of the mouse.

"Well, the lion thought the mouse's words were the
funniest he had ever heard. 'How can you, a tiny, wee
mouse, ever hope to help me, the King of Beasts?' the
lion asked, laughing. 'I think you are foolish, little mouse,
but because you have brightened my day I will let you go
free.'

"Many days passed, and one day the lion ventured
too close to the village, where a tribe of lion hunters
lived. His big paws sprang a trap, and a huge, strong net
fell from the trees and captured him. The lion roared in
agony and fear, thrashing about in the net, but only suc-
ceeding in trapping himself more tightly.

"Just as he was about to give up the struggle, the lion
heard the tiny squeak of a mouse. 'Live long, O King,'
the little mouse said. 'I am here to save your life as I promised.' And while the lion watched in amazement, the
mouse chewed away at the ropes until they unraveled,
and the lion walked free of the trap.

"And the lion learned," Kimberly said, smiling at the
little girl who had asked for the story, "that whether you

are big or small, you have the ability to help someone else."

The little girl smiled and closed her eyes to rest. Kimberly was about to do the same, but Brooke's nasal whine cut through the quiet: "Kimberly!"

She pulled her weight from the mast with an effort, and she doggedly trudged toward the place where Brooke lay near the window. As she passed by Thatcher, she accidentally allowed the wet edge of her kirtle to brush over his face.

"The devil take you!" Thatcher roared.

Stunned, Kimberly slowly turned around and realized what she'd done. Thatcher pushed himself up, leaning upon his elbows, and glared at her with chilling intentness for a long moment. "You're trying to bedevil me, Kimberly Hollis," he said, his voice clipped in anger. "Why don't you leave me alone?"

"Leave you alone?" Kimberly's emotions bobbed and spun like a piece of flotsam caught in the waves outside the ship. "Leave *you* alone? I am leaving you alone, for heaven's sake! Why would anyone want to be bothered with you? You're nothing but lazy, Thatcher Butler. You won't help with the younger ones. You won't do anything I ask you to. You're nothing but worthless scum, a crook, a criminal, riff-raff from the lowest London streets, the worst boy ever to have been born on the face of the earth—"

With difficulty she swallowed a hysterical surge of angry laughter. She wanted to cackle in his face, to tell him that his opinion meant nothing to her, that she really didn't care whether he helped her or not. But she reined in her temper and lifted her chin in what she hoped was a ladylike manner. "You are the most vile and disagreeable boy on this ship, Thatcher Butler," she said simply, then she turned on her heel and stepped away toward Brooke.

But his next words made her stop in her place: "Your mother didn't think so."

* * *

Darkness glided across the eastern sky with the silken slowness of the easygoing tide that moved against the ship. All around Kimberly, children slept, their bodies exhausted from the rigors of fighting a short but violent bout of sickness. Next to her, Christian and Ethan lay like dead men, for they were even more exhausted than the sick ones. They had done nothing but work since sunup, and Kimberly thought to herself that if Captain Blade were to give rewards for work well done, Ethan and Christian were certainly deserving.

She'd worked hard, too, but she couldn't sleep. Her muscles ached, her throat was parched with thirst, and her clothing clung to her sticky skin. But these things did not bother her as much as Thatcher's comment had. His words still rang in her mind. Though she tried to ignore him at the time, she could still hear his gentle taunt: "Your mother didn't think so."

She'd called him every horrible name she could think of. She'd insulted him thoroughly, and he deserved every word of it. But then he had talked about her mother. Why?

Kimberly drew her knees to her chest and rested her head on her arms. All day long she had tried to do what her mother would have done. She'd taken care of the younger ones, cleaned out the hold, kept the floors washed, taken the sick to fresh air. She'd done good work, but she couldn't feel pleased with herself because deep in her heart she knew she'd failed in one very important situation. Her mother would never have yelled at Thatcher the way Kimberly did. And Thatcher knew it.

A tear fell upon her cheek, and Kimberly brushed it away. "Why did you take my mother, God?" she whispered. "I'm trying to take her place, but I can't."

She listened for an answer in the quiet rhythm of the waves, but heard nothing.

202

Sunday, May 23

22

Thatcher groaned when the first rays of morning hit his face. The sun felt amazingly bright and hot on his eyelids, then he remembered that he'd been sick. Very sick. No wonder his body rebelled at the thought of morning.

He licked his parched lips and sat up. His stomach felt calmer now, and the tiny drums that had pounded inside his head were silent. Though he felt a bit weak and very hungry, he breathed a sigh of relief. He was better. No one would be bothering or fussing over him today.

The others seemed to have recovered, too, for no one leaned over the window, and the hold was much more quiet than it had been the day before. Yesterday had been a living nightmare, but through the agony of illness he'd felt one spark of real delight. He'd finally put Kimberly Hollis in her place. She called him a criminal and a thief, cutting him with her words, but he'd shut her up by mentioning her mother. Her face had grown pale, and she'd walked away, unable to answer him.

He stood on his shaky legs and moved to the window, eager for a breath of fresh air. Flat and dull, the sea spread itself before him like a spill of molten metal from a furnace. The ship rocked gently upon the surface, and in the shadows on the water Thatcher could see that the sails had been furled for the night. It was a brave sailor who dared sail through a clouded night sky, for readings were difficult to take without the stars, and a ship could easily be blown off course.

Thin puppetlike figures moved across the shadow ship in the water, and Thatcher watched as the crew prepared to make sail for another day. Where were they? he wondered. It would be easy to believe they had left the earth altogether and entered a world of wind, sky, and sea. Not a cloud marred the horizon this morning; there was nothing to see but the endless vista of blue water and sky.

Thatcher sank to his knees and leaned his elbows upon the windowsill. This was the life he would have chosen if he'd had the chance. Maybe it wasn't too late. If he could convince Captain Blade that he'd be of more use as a cabin boy or a sailor than an indentured servant, the captain might decide to keep Thatcher aboard the *Seven Brothers* and not sell him in Virginia. It was something to hope for, in any case.

204

A tiny speck suddenly appeared on the horizon, and Thatcher blinked and rubbed his eyes, afraid he was seeing things. Were his eyes playing tricks on him? He couldn't be sure, but the dark dot against the southern sky seemed to be growing larger.

"Sail ho!" the watchman cried from the deck above, and Thatcher's heart began to pound in his chest. Another ship! As it drew ever closer, Thatcher admired the vessel. Low and smooth in the water, she was, an elegant black caravel with square sails on her bowsprit and foremast and lateen sails on three other masts. He leaned forward upon the windowsill, loving the sun on his face and the sight of the ship on the horizon. If only he were the captain of such a vessel! She made good time across the sea, her sails billowing in the wind, her bow knifing through the water like a hot blade through butter. She was not as large as the bulky *Seven Brothers*, and Thatcher wished for a moment there was some way the two ships could race across the sea. He'd risk every coin in his poor breeches pocket betting on the beauty coming toward them!

Footsteps pounded on the deck overhead, but Thatcher ignored the sounds of his own ship's crew as he watched the sleek vessel painted against the brilliant sea. She was in truth a beauty, reminding him of the *Falcon Lady*—

Like the quick, chilling touch of a nightmare, fear shot through him. What if the approaching ship *was* the boat captained by Delmar de Chavez? Was he returning to take his revenge on Thatcher?

He froze at the window, his hands clenching the edge of the rough wooden sill, and did not notice that Wingate stood next to him until the other boy spoke. "Welladay, what's this? Has our captain's old friend come to visit us again?"

Thatcher stared at Wingate in a paralysis of astonishment. "You see it?" he asked, his voice cracking. "Is it truly the *Falcon Lady?*"

Wingate shrugged. "I don't know every ship in the sea, but I'd reckon so. Who else but Delmar de Chavez has a black ship with three-pointed sails?"

Thatcher turned back toward the sea. The strange ship was closer now and gaining fast. "Why do you suppose she's coming toward us?" he asked, hoping Wingate could provide a reasonable and reassuring answer.

But Wingate only frowned. "What makes you think that I would know that?"

* * *

On the other side of the ship, Kimberly dipped her hands and arms again into the bucket of water by the window. *'Tis good to have a bucket nearby*, she thought, *even if 'tis only filled with seawater. We should all wash our hands and faces every day. Methinks we'll be better spirited if we do.* She made a mental note to ask Squeege if they could keep a bucket in the hold, but a sudden shout from overhead distracted her thoughts.

"Off the port! There!" one of the seamen shouted, and Kimberly thought the crew pounded the deck above with unusual speed and vigor. Had they overslept? Or had they seen a storm on the southern horizon?

She frowned and glanced across the hold toward the other row of windows. They'd endured a terrible storm the night her mother died, and Kimberly didn't want to thrash through another one, especially after yesterday's spell of sickness. But the sky shone bold and blue through the windows on both sides of the ship. What, then, could have excited the seamen?

Wingate came toward her, a secretive smile on his face.

"I cry you mercy, speak," she sighed. She was stiff and sore and tired from taking care of the others and definitely not in a mood to play games.

"'Tis probably nothing," Wingate answered, leaning against the side of the ship. He folded his arms and grinned like a cat who'd just swallowed a bird. "But I saw the strangest thing just now. I've never seen the like before, and I'd wager I never will again."

"What could you have seen?" Kimberly asked, taking her hands out of the bucket of water. Her skin had begun to prune, so she dried her arms on her kirtle. "What could you have seen, Wingate, but clouds and water and lots of children—"

"I saw Thatcher."

"So? We all see more of him than we'd like to."

"He was affrightened."

"Thatcher?" She stopped wiping her hands. Thatcher was brassy, bold, cocky, arrogant, crude, and rude, but she couldn't imagine him being scared. What in the world could frighten Thatcher?

She cracked a smile. "He's pulling your leg, Wingate. What did he do, tell you he saw a sea monster?"

"Nay." Wingate shook his head. "We saw the *Falcon Lady*, Delmar de Chavez's ship. 'Tis south of us, and running before the wind like a bird. 'Twill be upon us before the day is out, I'd wager."

Kimberly felt her heart sink. "Oh no," she murmured. "If that man comes aboard again to get our captain drunk, we'll likely end up in India. We'll never make it to Virginia."

"Silly girl," Wingate chided. "Don't you know hundreds of the queen's best navigators are still looking for a western passage to India? We're not likely to find it."

"I care not about India. I only want to meet my father," Kimberly said, determined to change the subject. She pointed to the bucket of water. "Wash your hands and face. You should bathe every morning. I'm going to make everyone wash every day, and we'll take turns hauling up the water."

207

Wingate grinned good-naturedly and thrust his hands into the bucket. "So why do you think de Chavez is following us?" he asked, sloshing his hands in the water.

"Mayhap he's not," Kimberly answered. "Perchance he is en route to some other place."

"I think Thatcher fears that de Chavez is coming after *him*," Wingate whispered wickedly. His eyes gleamed with mischief. "The man looked most peculiarly at Thatcher when he came into the hold, and Thatcher did try to steal the man's purse."

"You're imagining things," Kimberly scolded. She

paused to listen to the activity overhead. "Albeit the seamen do seem a mite disturbed. Is it my imagination, or are they moving about more briskly than usual?"

Wingate lifted his eyes to the heavy planking over their heads as he and Kimberly listened. "All hands ahoy!" Squeege was shouting as the sailors rushed about. "Show a leg there, and spread that canvas. Step lively, or I'll run you up the yardarm and flog the pink off your bellies!"

"'Tis only the usual morning work," Wingate said, lifting his dripping hands out of the bucket. He moved toward Kimberly as if he would wipe his arms on her kirtle, but she sidestepped and wagged her finger at him.

"Nay, you'll not soil my kirtle with your dirty hands," Kimberly said, moving out of his way. Wingate looked about for a moment, then his eyes lit with laughter and he held his dripping fingers over Brooke Burdon's face as she slept.

"Oooo, that's cold," Brooke squealed, turning away from him as the other children laughed. Brooke was a late riser and usually lay sprawled asleep on the floor long after everyone else had risen. Now she blinked and sat up, then focused her glare on Wingate. "Why'd you spray me?"

208   "'Tis Kimberly's new rule," Wingate said, backing away. "Everyone must wash, and there's nothing to dry our hands."

Brooke transferred her angry gaze to Kimberly as Wingate left, but Kimberly ignored her and looked toward the port windows. Thatcher still stood there, his hands clinging to the side of the ship as if he feared he'd be tossed overboard at any moment. Past him, Kimberly could see the shape of a black ship on the horizon.

Was Delmar de Chavez really following them?

23

A tiny voice in Thatcher's head kept telling him to move away from the window, to go to the other side of the ship or hide in the small alcove at the stern. If he went away, so might the dark ship that had swept down like a vulture from the edge of the horizon. He could see the ship clearly now, could see men walking about on her deck under full-spread sails without a flag of any sort. The *Seven Brothers* sailed under the red, white, and blue British flag, displaying the Cross of St. George and the Cross of St. Andrew, but the dark vision that approached them now carried no flag at all. What kind of ship did not claim a country? Only one.

As if in answer to his thoughts, a dark blur began to shimmy up the forward mast of the caravel. Up, up it went, and when the wind spread it open, Thatcher saw a flag as black as the ship itself. A black flag meant one of two things: Either the ship had plague aboard and the flag was a warning not to venture near, or the vessel was filled with pirates who raised the flag as a boastful warning.

In the depths of his soul, Thatcher knew the reason for the *Falcon Lady's* black flag. Delmar de Chavez's ship bore no allegiance to any country because the pirate served only himself, looting and stealing and often sinking other ships upon the open sea.

The hard fist of fear grew in Thatcher's stomach. Thatcher had heard stories from seamen who came into London of murders on the high seas, of pirates who looted so thoroughly that the survivors were cast off without food, fresh water, or even sails to send their ships home. The unfortunate boats became ghost ships, drifting until the passengers perished or a storm sent them to the bottom of the deep.

He couldn't tell the others. They'd know the horrible truth soon enough. He glanced around, frantic to find something he could use to defend himself in case the pirates came aboard. Most cargo ships carried cannons on this second deck, but Captain Blade had removed the guns to make room for the children. Thatcher closed his eyes. He remembered seeing several small guns on the upper deck, but they would be no match for a well-equipped pirate ship.

As if de Chavez could read Thatcher's mind from across the water, a puff of smoke rose from the black ship's bow, followed in half a heart's beat by the deep boom of the cannon that had fired it. The sea between the two vessels spat up in a white plume, and every head in the hold lifted toward the sound. Thatcher could *feel* the others' fear.

"What was that, Thatcher?" a tiny voice came to him. He turned around. A little girl, probably not more than eight years old, stood behind him with her finger in her mouth. Her eyes were wide with worry, her face pale and drawn.

"'Twas nothing," he answered, moving away from the window. He saw Kimberly and Wingate frozen in place like statues on the other side of the ship. *If Miss Hollis wants to be a leader*, Thatcher thought, *'tis time for her to behave as one.*

* * *

Kimberly paused at the booming sound. "Thunder?" she asked, turning to Christian.

"Nay," the blind boy answered, tilting his head toward the south. "More like a big gun. Someone has fired a cannon."

"Why?" Kimberly asked, her mouth going dry. She looked across the hold toward the opposite windows. Thatcher had left his post and was coming her way while men's footsteps pounded the deck above in an uneven rhythm.

Thatcher's face was grim when he looked at her. "Why would another ship fire a cannon?" she asked, half afraid of the answer.

"'Twas a warning," Thatcher said, keeping his voice low. He gestured toward the corner, and Kimberly led Christian away from the younger children huddled near them. "I don't want to frighten the little ones," Thatcher said, his eyes more serious than Kimberly had ever seen them. "But the ship out there flies a black flag."

"Plague?" Christian asked.

"Pirates," Thatcher answered. "They fired a cannon and they're coming up fast, so my guess is that they are preparing to board us."

"Board—this ship?" Kimberly shrieked, forgetting herself. Several of the younger children looked her way, alarmed, and she forced herself to smile at them as if it were all a joke. When they were satisfied and had gone

211

back to their conversations, she turned again to Thatcher. "Why would they want to board this ship?" she demanded in an intense whisper. "What have we got but dry biscuits? Captain Blade has no treasure or gold aboard."

"You forget," Ethan said, joining them. "We're worth our weight in gold, remember? That's what Captain Blade told Delmar de Chavez."

"De Chavez wanted more than anything to know what our cargo was," Thatcher said. "That's why he told that foolish story about being the captain's long-lost friend. He got the captain drunk just to have a little look in the *Seven Brothers'* hold."

"At us," Kimberly murmured, a whisper of terror running through her. "We're the cargo."

"Worth our weight in tobacco, which is as good as gold," Ethan answered, his brows a brooding knot over his eyes.

Kimberly sank to her knees, then sat down in a stunned huddle. It was unthinkable that she should be nothing but a valuable piece of cargo. Aboard the *Seven Brothers* she and her mother had been paying passengers, and though now she traveled alone like the other children, still she thought of herself as different. She wasn't destined for indentured service. She had a ticket out of this nightmarish life, a father who would take her to freedom.

But if a pirate took them all, she'd be just like the others. *Cargo.* Not a person, not a daughter, but worth eighty-two pounds of tobacco.

"This can't happen," she said, reaching up to grasp Thatcher's hand. His eyes met hers, and she saw for the first time that he was as frightened as she. "They can't come aboard this ship, Thatcher, they just can't. Doesn't the captain have cannons, too?"

"A few," Thatcher said. "Not many. And they're not

very big guns. I don't think he expected anyone to bother a ship filled with young'uns."

"De Chavez can't take us," Kimberly said, her panic rising. "By heaven, someone has to stop him! Why, he'll carry us to some godforsaken place and sell us to strangers who don't care anything about us, people who might be cruel and harsh—"

She turned to Ethan for help, but saw a mingling of pity and accusation in his eyes. She frowned—what had she said to upset him? But as her own words echoed in her brain, she realized what she had said. She was terrified beyond reason by the very thing the other children faced whether they stayed with Captain Blade or were captured by the pirates.

"Oh," she said, pulling her hand from Thatcher's grasp. She bit her lip as her cheeks burned. She'd imagined Captain Blade as a friend, but in truth, he was a kidnapper and as much a pirate as Delmar de Chavez.

"I only hope he doesn't sink us," Thatcher said, his voice hoarse with fear. "If Blade doesn't surrender and we're broadsided by a cannonball, we'll go down faster than lightning."

"He wouldn't sink us," Ethan said, spreading his hands. "We're too valuable a cargo. He'd take us off first, then sink the ship."

213

"Nay," Thatcher said, shaking his head. "De Chavez is cruel. He told Squeege that I was a thief because he knew a thief when he saw one. He said my heart was as black as any knave's."

"That wasn't very kind," Ethan said, blinking.

"He knew I was a thief because he's a thief," Thatcher answered, pounding the air with his fist. "He saw that I was like him. Only he's meaner than me, I promise. If my heart's black, then his is—" he struggled for a word—"his heart's a chunk of coal."

"You're right," Kimberly whispered, surprised that

Thatcher had just admitted that he was a scoundrel. She stood to her feet. "But things might get rough here, and the men above will be too busy to bother with us. We'll have to keep the little ones quiet and away from the windows. Mayhap if we all crowd onto this side of the hold . . ."

She raised her hand to gesture toward the starboard windows, but suddenly the trapdoor above opened and half a dozen seamen barrelled down the narrow stairs, barely touching the steps. They pressed through the hold as children scrambled out of their way, then they lifted the hatch that led to the lower hold and disappeared down the companion ladder into the dim light below.

"What do ye think they're doing?" Thatcher asked, standing on tiptoe to peer over the others' heads. In a moment, the answer came. The seamen reappeared, hauling up supplies. Without wasting a moment they passed the barrels and casks from one to another in a line until the last sailor tossed the supplies out the window and into the sea.

"Don't we need that food?" Kimberly asked as a steady stream of containers splashed into the ocean. She peered out the window. The *Seven Brothers* was moving faster, plunging her bow and raising her stern like a wild horse surprised to be ridden so hard so early in the day. Behind the ship a path of bobbing trunks and casks pebbled the surface of the sea.

"They're lightening the load," Thatcher explained, his face grim. "Trying to outrun the pirates. They'll only toss overboard what we don't need—unless the captain grows desperate."

"Dear God in heaven, help us," Kimberly breathed, scarcely believing the sight before her eyes.

As the seamen jettisoned supplies out of the north-facing starboard windows, children lined the south-facing port windows and cheered the captain on. "He's coming! Hurry, Captain Blade, hurry! He's coming!"

Kimberly stared at the freakish scene and felt the hold swirl around her. Without thinking, she reached out to cling to Thatcher's shoulders as barrels continued to splash overboard and the wind blew the *Seven Brothers* away from her pursuer. The sails above flapped and creaked, the ship groaned, waves splashed, the floor dipped and rose beneath her feet as the ship bucked through the water. Faster. Faster. Oh, please, God, make it go faster. Looking toward the south, Kimberly could see the black ship clearly, the pirate's flag fluttering high on her mainmast, her black bow cutting cleanly through the water. Men stood ready on her decks, the morning sun glinting off the drawn swords in their hands.

A cannon boomed, and the splash fell only a few feet short of the window where the children watched. They screamed and scrambled away from the opening, and Kimberly knew the next shot would not fall short.

"Dear God," she cried, releasing Thatcher's shoulders as she slipped to her knees. "I'm sorry for ever thinking I was better than the others. Help us now, please!"

* * *

A sudden gust of wind spurred the *Seven Brothers* forward, and Kimberly opened her eyes in gratitude. Had God answered her prayer?

The stairs of the companionway squeaked in protest as Squeege lumbered into the hold. "Ye young'uns stay away from the window," he called, gesturing toward the center of the ship. "Stay near the masts if ye can."

"Are we going to get away?" Brooke asked, her voice a terrified treble.

"Aye, we'll outrun the varmints," Squeege said, glancing around. He called to the other seamen who were

215

still hauling barrels up from the lower hold. "Don't pitch any more, lads. Have we enough provisions remaining?"

A sailor poked his head through the opening. "We've enough for three weeks, mayhap four if we ration the food and water," he called.

"Good," Squeege said. "Come back up to the deck, for the captain's going to need every hand to man the sheets. We're going to outrun the devils."

As the seamen climbed out of the lower hold, Kimberly's eyes met Thatcher's. His eyes were like black holes in his pale face, deep wells of feeling she couldn't begin to understand.

"Kimberly," Christian called, his voice cutting through the sound of the sailor's footsteps, "has anyone thought about dinner? I hate to mention it at such a time, but now that we're safely away I believe I must. My own stomach is cramping in hunger, and I can imagine how everyone else must feel."

"You're right, Christian. We need something to eat," Kimberly answered, grateful for a chance to think about something other than the pirates in the distance. "Yesterday we didn't eat a thing. If the men are to be up on deck, someone's got to feed us—"

216   "Who?" Thatcher asked, lifting an eyebrow.

She stared at him in frustration. It was just like Thatcher to question her without offering help. "I'll go get something myself," she said, lifting her kirtle as she rose to her feet. Thatcher said nothing, but grinned at her as she sidestepped over the rolling deck toward the opening that led to the lower hold.

"Do you need help?" Ethan asked, appearing at her elbow.

"Yea," she answered, turning to climb down the stair-case that led below. "And thank you, Ethan. You're the only one I can count on these days."

The three bilge boys were happy to open a barrel of

sea biscuits, but Kimberly crinkled her nose when she peered inside. Little gray tufts of fuzz adorned the hard, circular biscuits, and she poked a timid finger inside the barrel. "What's this fuzz?" she asked, looking toward one of the bilge boys.

He peeked inside and then shrugged. "Those are naught but spiders' webs," he said. "They make nests in the barrels."

"Spiders' nests?" Kimberly gave Ethan a suspicious sideways squint. "We've been eating biscuits covered by *spiders' nests?*"

The bilge boy shrugged. "We clean 'em off before we bring 'em out. We usually get most of the gray stuff off."

Kimberly felt her mouth go dry. She didn't want to eat these biscuits or anything else, but common sense told her that she and the others had to eat. The sick ones were weak, and she could feel her own energy draining away. If they were to survive this terrible day, they'd have to eat whatever was aboard the ship.

"Help me with these," she told Ethan, reaching into the barrel for a handful of the dusty-looking biscuits. She rubbed one of them on her kirtle to wipe away the fuzzy gray webbing, and a score of little red spiders skittered out and wriggled across the fabric of her dress.

217

Her heart thumped against her rib cage at the sight of so many squirming spiders, but Ethan quickly brushed the critters from her kirtle. "We've got to do this, Kimberly," he said, his hand closing firmly about her elbow. "Come on, we'll wipe these on my breeches and use your kirtle to hold them. Just don't faint on me."

"I won't," she managed to whisper. Ethan grabbed another handful of the biscuits, wiped away the gray, and began to toss them into her kirtle as she held it up like a basket.

* * *

Kimberly was glad for the modesty of her petticoat as she moved through the hold giving biscuits to the other children. Most of them took the dry biscuit with gratitude and nibbled on it slowly, as if they somehow knew that food had become precious. In the back of her mind, Kimberly realized that the dry biscuits were probably a very good dinner for children who had been sick with queasy stomachs. And she would definitely not tell them about the spiders.

When she had finished serving the others, Kimberly sat next to Ethan near the bow and tried not to look out the window. She could still see the black ship behind them, as persistent as a pesky mosquito. Captain Blade had pushed the *Seven Brothers* to a fast clip, but the *Falcon Lady* had not given up her pursuit. Though out of cannon range, she remained steady on the horizon, neither gaining or losing in the race.

Kimberly nudged Ethan, then nodded toward the window. "Do you think he's unable to catch up, or unwilling?" she asked, taking care to keep her voice low so she wouldn't alarm the others. "Is de Chavez playing games with us?"

218   Ethan pressed his lips together. "I don't know much about the sea," he said, raking his hand through his curly hair. "But I know our captain doesn't like to sail in darkness, and the day is nearly spent. I fear that the pirates may be waiting for us to furl our sails for the night."

"Why couldn't we sail through the night?" Kimberly asked, panic rising in her throat. "The wind will still blow—"

"'Tis a risk if the skies are clouded," Ethan pointed out. "The captain has only the stars to steer the ship, and if he cannot see them, he will not know where he's going. A mad rush might lead us into a trap, dangerous waters, or a storm. Captain Blade has to keep his wits about him."

"May God help us," Kimberly said, her pulse quickening as she noticed the lengthening shadows in the hold. The sun would sink before long, and if the captain took in the sails . . .

The upper hatch squeaked, and Squeege again thundered his way through the hold. Behind him followed another half-dozen seamen. They did not speak to the children, but proceeded to enter the lower hold and haul up additional barrels of supplies. Kimberly stared at the brigade in hypnotized horror. Did they not realize how much food they were tossing to the waves?

"Are you going to throw everything overboard?" Thatcher asked, confronting Squeege. "We have to eat, you know—"

"Would you like us to throw you overboard instead of these barrels?" Squeege interrupted, his eyes glowing in determination. "If you give me any more trouble, I might as well."

Thatcher didn't back down. "What does it matter if we serve as slaves on this ship or on that yonder one?" he asked, pointing out the window. "But we'll starve if you keep pitching our food into the sea."

Squeege growled, but he held up his hand, and the two seamen at the window paused before tilting a huge barrel into the ocean.

219

Kimberly sighed in relief. For once, she had to admit, Thatcher had done something good.

* * *

Thatcher spent the next hour pacing before the windows. The *Seven Brothers* pushed on in a valiant effort, and by the time the sun set there was no sign of the dark pirate ship on the water. The ocean stood empty and vast, with nothing between the captives' ship and the bloodred horizon colored by the setting sun.

"We outran them," Ethan said, satisfaction in his

voice. "Captain Blade can rest easy now. We'll sleep well tonight."

Thatcher wasn't certain he would ever sleep well again, but he didn't dispute Ethan's confident words. He lay down close by the window and often sat up to scan the horizon for any sign of the dark *Falcon Lady*.

Captain Blade sailed for at least an hour after dark, then Thatcher heard him call the order to furl the sheets. Clouds covered the night sky, obscuring the moon and stars, and the ship settled into the easy rocking motion of a boat at rest. Lulled by the sound and rhythm of the water, Thatcher fell into a shallow doze.

He didn't know if he slept for hours or minutes, but a different sound suddenly woke him. He sat up, alarmed. What was that whooshing noise? He strained to hear. Another noise floated across the water—music. The sound of singing. Voices. Was he dreaming?

As the others slept around him, Thatcher rose to his knees and peered over the edge of the windowsill. It was difficult to see anything in the clouded gray night, but he thought a dark form loomed out on the water.

The wind blew, the clouds parted, and in a sudden shaft of moonlight Thatcher saw the ship. The *Falcon Lady* rode the waters only a few feet away, close enough for him to hear the sounds of merriment and music from within the lower cabin. Thatcher crinkled his nose. He thought he could almost *smell* the pirates, the aroma of their cook fire, and the cheap scent of perfume upon their captain's clothes.

Delmar de Chavez had returned like a terrible nightmare and would be waiting when the sun arose.

220

Monday, May 24

24

Awareness hit Kimberly like a punch in the stomach as the first rays of light filtered into the hold. She opened her eyes and sat up, knowing full well what she'd see when she looked out the window. She had heard the pirate ship in the night; she thought she could even smell the whiskey de Chavez's men were drinking. But she hadn't said anything to the others.

Now she closed her eyes and prayed. "Heavenly Father," she whispered, making an effort to keep her thoughts directed heavenward instead of worrying about what lay outside the ship, "we need you again. Yesterday you sent the wind so we could outrun the pirates, but today they are right outside the window."

A sound like the clanging of steel distracted her thoughts, then she heard a familiar voice call across the waters: "Ahoy, Captain Blade! I wait to have a word with you!"

Kimberly refused to open her eyes, but prayed harder. "Father God," she whispered, clenching her fists, "I know I was wrong. All through this journey I've seen myself as someone special and thought I ought to be in charge. I didn't serve the others out of love. I led them because I thought I was *better* somehow, knowing I wouldn't have to face the auction block—"

"What is it you want, de Chavez?" Captain Blade bellowed from above. Still with her eyes closed, Kimberly could hear the children around her draw expectant breaths as they listened. The showdown between the two captains had begun.

"God, I'll never think of myself as superior again," Kimberly promised. "But keep your hand of protection upon us today, please. And show me what I must do now to help."

She opened her eyes. The other children sat in quiet rows, their faces tight with apprehension as they watched the windows. They could not see Captain Blade above them, but Delmar de Chavez pirouetted before their eyes on the deck of his ship. He carried a sword in one hand and a pistol in the other, and the black mouths of three large cannons loomed from portholes in the side of his ship.

222

The *Falcon Lady* was quite close, close enough for Kimberly to see the creases in de Chavez's face. "I've chased you all I'm going to," the pirate called to Captain Blade. "And now it ends. Stand down, Captain, and prepare to be boarded."

Kimberly took a deep breath and sat back. She'd asked God to help them, and she'd confessed her terrible sin of pride. There was nothing to do now but sit and wait for God's will to be done.

* * *

From his place near the window, Thatcher felt his mouth go dry. Would Captain Blade stand aside and let that pirate take over the ship? That would certainly mean Captain Blade's death if he did, for no pirate would let a rival captain live. So Captain Blade might choose to fight, and if he did, those cannons would fire straight into the hold. The ship would go down in a matter of minutes.

Thatcher imagined the pain of a cannon ball landing squarely in his middle. He grimaced, and the memory of the pirate's last words to him passed through him like an unwelcome chill. "Till we meet again," de Chavez had said, smiling at Thatcher, and now they *would* meet unless some miracle prevented it.

He glanced over at Kimberly Hollis. She'd be the type to pray for a miracle, and he half expected to see her on her knees with her hands clasped and her face lifted as she babbled a prayer. But she sat quietly, her hands in her lap, her eyes on the window beyond. The expression on her face was different, though. Thatcher couldn't believe it, but in her eyes he saw peace.

How could she be so calm in the face of disaster? She had been frantic when the pirates first appeared, when the others were sick, and when her mother died. But today she sat as calmly as if she were in church, her eyes wide and trusting like her mother's.

The same peaceful calm had filled Mistress Hollis's eyes, even through the worst of her pain. Right before she died, Thatcher saw her turn those trusting eyes upon Kimberly and promise that the family would be reunited soon.

Was that why Kimberly was so calm? Had God told her they'd all be in heaven before the day's end? Against his will, Thatcher's feet dragged him to Kimberly, and he knelt beside her, his eyes fastened to the confident glow on her face.

223

* * *

Kimberly was surprised to see Thatcher at her side. His face was taut with fear, his hands clasped together as if he were trying to keep them from shaking. "What will happen here today?" he whispered. "Do you know?"

The corner of her mouth drooped in a half smile. "Do I know?" she asked, lifting an eyebrow. "How would I know such a thing?"

"You don't look frightened," Thatcher said, clearing his throat nervously. His eyes darted around the hold, then flew to the window. "And believe me, there's much to be frightened of out there on the sea. Delmar de Chavez makes Captain Blade look like a saint."

Kimberly smiled in the calm strength of knowledge. "God makes both men look like mere ants," she said, lifting her chin. "I have prayed, Thatcher. Yesterday, when it seemed that all was lost, God sent a wind and blew us away from the pirates. Today he will work again."

"No wind's going to get us away this time," Thatcher said. "Our sails are furled. Before we'd have time to raise the sheets, the *Falcon Lady's* cannons would blow holes in our hull."

Kimberly lifted her shoulder in an elegant shrug. "It doesn't matter. I don't know why we're in this spot, but God will have his way." She paused, not wanting to fill Thatcher with false hope. "I don't know whether God 224 wants us on this ship or that one," she said, pointing out the window. "It may well be that we are taken onto the *Falcon Lady* before this day is over."

"And you're happy about that?"

She shook her head. "Nay. I wouldn't be happy about it. But I'm not going to worry about myself anymore. God will do what is best for all of us. In that I am confident. Whatever happens, God will work his plan."

Thatcher lowered his head onto his hand, and she gentled her voice. "What brings you to me, Thatcher? You've never come to me for advice before."

He shook his head, unwilling to speak, but as the two captains continued to threaten each other, Thatcher met her eyes. "'Twas the look on your face," he said, his voice heavy and sad. "Your mother wore the same look. She gave me hope."

"And why do you need hope?"

He snorted at the question. "Isn't it obvious?" He flung his hands toward the open windows. "De Chavez hates me. Captain Blade dislikes me. Even you have said I'm a crook and criminal, a blackhearted knave worthy of nothing."

Kimberly felt the sting of her conscience. "I was wrong," she whispered. "'Tis not my place to judge you. My heart is of certain not the purest on God's earth."

He looked at her, surprised, and Kimberly gave him a slow smile. "I've had to clean my own heart in the last day. That's why my face looks like my mother's. God has forgiven me of my own sinful pride."

"Oh yes? Well, God of certain hates me, else why would he have taken my mother and yours? He can't forgive me for what I've done. If I hadn't tried to snatch de Chavez's purse back at the Azores, none of this would have happened. I've brought this evil upon us all, and if Captain Blade and the others are killed, their blood will be on my hands!"

"God doesn't hate you, Thatcher," Kimberly said, silently praying that God would give her the wisdom to know what to say. "And if you think your mother's death is proof that God hates you, then he must hate me, too, for my mother is in heaven with him."

Thatcher didn't answer, but sat silently, listening.

"God loves us both, and he can forgive you for whatever you've done if you're willing to come to him in repentance. My mother died because she was sick, but God has not left me alone or without comfort. He has put me on a ship filled with friends, and he will continue to hold my life in his hands no matter what happens."

"So that's why you're so calm," Thatcher said slowly. "You can accept anything?"

"Yea," she answered. "'Tisn't always easy, for certain, but I trust God always. And I know that if I mourn, I will be comforted." She reached out and placed her hand on Thatcher's shoulder. "You can be happy if you mourn for your sin and accept God's comfort. 'Tis easily done, Thatcher. I know, for I've had to do it often enough."

"You?" His short laugh was bitter.

"Yea. Anyone. For God doesn't see us as we are once we ask his pardon. He sees us as we can be."

* * *

Kimberly's words echoed in Thatcher's brain. *He sees us as we can be!* That was how Mistress Hollis saw him when she said he was special. He sat for a moment in pleased surprise, and hope poked through the surface of his hardened heart like blades of grass in the springtime. If God had power enough to change him, of certain God had power enough to defeat the evil intentions of Delmar de Chavez. If he could only trust God like Kimberly did.

"Prepare to be boarded or to be sent to the depths of the deep," de Chavez called, the teasing challenge completely gone from his voice. "My patience wears thin, and I am ready to take the prize. I'd rather take your ship, Blade, and keep the brats on board, but if I have to sink her, I will."

"They can't swim," Captain Bladé answered, his voice flat. "If you sink us, you'll lose most of the children."

Delmar de Chavez shrugged. "I'll pluck as many as I can from the water and send the rest to the bottom with you," he said. He motioned with his sword, and the sun's rays glimmered off the blade. "Lower your shallop and prepare to receive me."

Thatcher jerked in surprise when Kimberly stood abruptly and moved to the far side of the ship, away from the scene unfolding at the port windows. Had de Chavez's threat shaken her faith? Thatcher stood to follow her, but froze when he heard Captain Blade's next words.

"I won't lower the shallop."

De Chavez's face darkened in anger, and he thrust his sword down at his side. "Very well. Prepare to die."

Thatcher turned toward Kimberly. "Kimberly—"

"You know, there's a story in the Bible," she said, staring at the open sea through the starboard windows. "Elijah prayed that God would show his power by sending rain when there had been none for three years."

"That's good, Kimberly," Thatcher said, his attention distracted by the sight of the pirates scurrying over their ship in preparation for the attack.

"And Elijah sent his servant to look for rain. The servant had to go look toward the sea seven times, but on the seventh time he told his master that he saw a little cloud the size of a man's hand."

Thatcher felt the blood drain from his face. Had Kimberly lost her mind? While she rambled senselessly about clouds and servants, from where he stood he could see de Chavez's men loading a heavy iron ball into the biggest cannon. The gun was aimed straight toward him.

"I see it, too," Kimberly called from the far window.

"You see it?" Thatcher said, his eyes still fastened to the cannon. When de Chavez gave the order, they would light the fuse. In another moment it would be all over. Was this what Kimberly meant when she said God would work his will? Was it his plan that they join him in heaven before dinner?

"The cloud," Kimberly said. "Only 'tis bigger than a man's hand. 'Tis more like a serpent, and 'tis coming this way."

Ethan suddenly jumped from his place. "May the Master of the Universe be praised!" he shouted, running

227

to Kimberly's window. He thrust his hand toward the sea, pointing. "Look! Our salvation approaches!"

Thatcher tore his eyes from the awesome sight of the cannon and looked toward the open sea. A dark, funnel-shaped cloud had arisen as if from nowhere, and its long tongue licked the surface of the sea, spewing water as it moved steadily toward them.

Ethan stared toward the cloud. "'The voice of the Lord is upon the waters: the God of glory thundereth: the Lord is upon many waters,'" he quoted, his voice reverent and strangely musical in the stillness of the hold. "'The Lord sitteth upon the flood; yea, the Lord sitteth King for ever.'"

A sailor up on the deck screamed a warning. "Waterspout off the starboard bow!" Footsteps pounded overhead like thunder, and the gray whirlwind pirouetted and swayed across the face of the deep. The sky above began to churn and boil, and Thatcher shivered as darkness thickened and congealed around him.

"What has God done?" he wondered aloud. His mind kept trying to say things to his body—he ought to duck, to run, to hide—but his eyes would not leave the black, snaking monster cloud that now roared over the ocean with a strength of sound and wind he had never imagined.

"Get down!" Kimberly screamed, running into the center of the ship. She threw herself on top of two young ones, pulling them down to the deck with her, and Thatcher had only a moment to glance at the pirate ship before he staggered to his knees. The pirates who had been taunting them only a moment before stood like stone, frozen in absolute horror. The monster cloud spun toward the *Seven Brothers*, rose into the air like a whirling top, then fell upon the pirate ship and ripped the foremast from the deck with no more effort than if it had been the slightest sliver of wood. A wall of whirling water

228

suddenly rose around the *Falcon Lady*, and the force of the moving sea pushed the *Seven Brothers* firmly away from the fury of the raging whirlwind.

Children screamed, and Thatcher fell forward upon the deck, burying his head in his hands. He fully expected at any moment to feel the ocean pouring in upon him, but though the wind howled in rage and the sea rose up to snarl at them, not a drop of water came through the open windows.

After a few anxious moments, Thatcher lifted his head. Several children whimpered in fear from where they lay, but all was silent on the deck overhead. He shivered. Had the entire crew been washed overboard?

25

Thatcher stood to his shaky feet and moved to the companionway. Gripping the rail firmly, he climbed upward and pushed on the hatch. It fell open with a loud thud, and he climbed slowly, afraid that he would find a broken and deserted ship.

He peered over the edge of the deck. All three masts still stood, the ship's sails neatly furled upon the yards. On the deck four and twenty seamen stood or sat, their eyes open wide and their faces ashen. They had seen the awesome power of God's deliverance, and yet they did not believe.

"Ahoy up here," Thatcher called, his voice cracking. "Are we all accounted for?"

Squeege turned toward Thatcher, and the big man's face was the color of parchment. "Aye, every man is still with us," the bosun said, shaking his head as if he could not trust his senses. "I don't know what happened, but we're still among the land of the living."

Thatcher felt his knees grow weak. Kimberly Hollis had prayed for a miracle, and by heaven, she'd received one. Though later the sailors would say it was just a rogue waterspout, Thatcher knew better. Why would a whirlwind skip one ship and attack another?

"'Twas a frightful thing," he said, searching for words to fill the awkward silence. "How fares the captain?"

Squeege jerked his thumb toward the captain's cabin. "See to him, will you, boy? I don't think me legs are ready for walking yet."

Thatcher climbed out of the companionway and slowly walked over the deck toward the small door of the captain's cabin. Hesitantly, he knocked.

"Enter," a voice called, and Thatcher pushed the door open. Captain Blade sat on the edge of his bunk, his face pale and his eyes red. His hands hung uselessly in his lap, and his long hair was disheveled. He lifted weary eyes to Thatcher's face. "Is there trouble below?" he asked, speaking in the low voice grownups reserved for dreaded topics. "Did we lose any of the children?"

"Not a soul," Thatcher answered, smiling. "'Twas the most amazing thing, Captain—"

232 "I have never seen anything like it," Blade said, shaking his head. "Not in all my years at sea. I wasn't afraid of de Chavez, mind you, and was prepared to fight for my ship, but the sight of that killer cloud turned my knees to jelly." Something flickered far back in the captain's eyes. "I thought both ships were doomed, truth to tell. And then the power of the beast flew above our heads and took the caravel, and something shoved us out of the way even though our sails were furled. 'Twas like a mighty hand, I tell you, pushing us along the water so fast that my men had to hold onto the masts to keep from being blown over the edge."

"I think I can explain," Thatcher said, unable to

keep the truth to himself. "'Twas all an act of God. Kimberly Hollis was praying, you see, and right when de Chavez was about to blow us out of the water, she said something about a cloud the size of a man's hand. She said God had done something like this before, in the Bible, and something about a servant and no rain for three years—" Thatcher broke off, knowing that his words were hopelessly confused. "But then the cloud was upon us, and I felt our ship rushing away. And I saw the cloud and the water take the pirate ship, and her masts broke like that—" He snapped his fingers.

"Why not us?" Captain Blade asked, lifting an eyebrow.

Thatcher shrugged. "I don't know. And though Kimberly had prayed, she said she didn't know if we'd survive the day or not. But she was confident and said God would work his will."

The captain's face cracked into a rueful smile. "Is it God's will that we have jettisoned most of our supplies? That we have very little food and fresh water? We don't even know of certain that the pirate ship was destroyed, and for all we know she will be back to finish us off within the week. If this is God's protection, my boy . . ."

233

Thatcher shook his head. "I don't understand it either, sir. All I know is what Kimberly said. And she didn't seem at all surprised when that cloud fell out of the sky. And she wasn't at all afraid when de Chavez pointed his cannons right at us." He paused and looked down at his feet. "God has given us his protection. Mayhap 'tis his will that we trust him for the things we lack."

The captain didn't answer, but regarded Thatcher with a frankly doubtful glance. "I suppose I'd better get back down to the hold," Thatcher said, moving toward the door. He forced a laugh. "I just had to make sure we still had a crew to pilot this ship."

"Aye, we do," Captain Blade answered. "Though I'm not sure I understand why."

Thatcher left the captain sitting in a daze and returned to the hold.

* * *

Sunlight had filled the hold when he returned, and the younger children scampered about and chattered as if nothing had happened. Outside the ship, the late morning air was washed with brilliance and canopied by a clean blue sky. Not a cloud lingered, not even in the distance. 'Twas as if they had been pushed into another world.

Thatcher took a deep breath of the clean air and exulted in the warm kernel of happiness that occupied the center of his being. Never in his life had he felt so free. After what he had seen today, he knew he should never worry about anything again. More than that, Kimberly Hollis had taught him not to worry about his past, his reputation, or his own fears about what he might become. What did it matter that de Chavez had called him a blackhearted knave? De Chavez's own heart was so darkened by evil that it was doubtful he could see good in anyone. But Mistress Hollis had seen a glimmer of goodness in Thatcher, and he was determined to live up to her expectations for him.

Feeling unusually awkward and shy, he moved toward Kimberly and waited for a space to open up near her. When one of the smaller children stood and moved away, he slipped into the spot and smiled when she looked at him in surprise.

"What's this?" she asked, lifting a brow. "Have you something of import to tell me?"

"Only this," he said, lifting one knee and wrapping his arms around it. "I thought I might help you keep the younger ones entertained. I know 'tis a big job."

"Yea," she said, her eyes lit with quiet laughter. "And how do you propose to help me?"

"I could tell my favorite memory," he said, looking at the young faces around Kimberly. "'Twas a night we passed right here on this ship. I was restless, and Kimberly's blessed mother lay her hand upon mine and told me I was special. I didn't believe her then, but I've come to believe her now."

He glanced at Kimberly to see her reaction. She didn't say anything, but her eyes glistened with tears and a shy smile played upon her lips.

"So, what's your favorite memory, Kimberly?" he asked, teasing. "With all that's happened, I'd wager you have a new one."

"Yea, tell us, Kimberly!" the other children chorused, urging her on.

"I can't," she finally said, blushing, and Thatcher noticed for the first time how pretty Kimberly Hollis was. Her face shone like gold in the warm sunlight reflecting off the water, and high cheekbones accented her warm brown eyes. A light dusting of freckles upon her cheeks gave her a soft, down-to-earth look.

"Why can't you tell it?" Thatcher asked, leaning forward. 235

"Because I think 'tis happening right now," she said, blushing to the roots of her hair. She spread her hands and smiled around the circle. "All of you—here—now. After all we've been through, this particular moment is bound to be one of my favorite memories."

Leaning back on his elbows, Thatcher found her words very encouraging.

* * *

Later that day, when the excitement of the storm had passed, Kimberly found Ethan sitting by the window in his usual position of prayer. She quietly sank down beside him and listened to the words of the prophet Isaiah he quoted: "'And in that day thou shalt say, O Lord, I will praise thee: though thou wast angry with me, thine anger is turned away, and thou comfortedst me. Behold, God is my salvation; I will trust, and not be afraid: for the Lord Jehovah is my strength and my song; he also is become my salvation.'"

"Amen," she whispered, grateful to God for the miracles of the past days.

But what would tomorrow bring?